BULLET RAIN

BULLET RAIN

Robert Swartwood

RMS Press

ISBN-13: 978-1945819018
ISBN-10: 1945819014

www.robertswartwood.com

Dedicated to my grandmother, Audrey Acton
August 5, 1926 — April 18, 2014

BULLET RAIN

1

The sniper sat on top of the ridge, his back against a boulder. He had his eyes closed, earbuds in his ears, listening to an audiobook.

He listened to an audiobook almost every day, having nothing else to do except sit here in this makeshift hut and wait. There was a cooler with water and Gatorade and the remains of his lunch—tuna fish sandwich and barbecue potato chips, a can of diet soda—and that was it. If he needed to loosen his bowels, he did so in a hole one hundred yards away.

His transportation was a 2009 Honda CRF dirt bike. It was parked five hundred yards away down the embankment, in the shade of a Utah juniper tree.

In the next hour or so he would ride the dirt bike three miles across the desert to town. His home, a doublewide trailer, sat on the outskirts. A wooden shed was beside it, and it was into the shed he would ease the dirt bike, snap shut the padlock on the door, and head inside the trailer. Strip out of his clothes, take a shower, then lower himself down into his recliner with a cold bottle of beer, turn on the TV, and watch sports until he drifted off to sleep.

But that was later, and this was now, and currently he sat with his back against the boulder, his eyes closed, listening to his audiobook. It was a murder mystery, a book in an ongoing series that he liked. What he liked most was the narrator's voice. It was smooth and confident. The narrator had the uncanny ability to change his voice to match any character in the book, even a secondary character, sometimes even a tertiary character.

The sniper was impressed.

He was also bored.

This job paid well—exceedingly well—and it was relatively easy, but not much happened. Hence the earbuds and audiobook. Hence the hut with the corrugated steel roof that protected him from the sun. The desert was dry and played hell on his sinuses, but he had become accustomed to it over the past two years. That was how long he had been doing the work, ever since he had left the Marines.

He had had thirty-seven kills during his service to his country.

He was a killer, he supposed, though he thought of himself more as a marksman. A very *skilled* marksman, to be exact, one of the best in his platoon, so it made sense why he had been snatched up so quickly after leaving the Marines.

Of course, the fact that he had a gambling problem, and that he had been down nearly one hundred thousand dollars, also factored into his decision to be where he was right now.

His debt had been paid off long ago, and if he wanted, he could have left this job and pursued another, but hell, the money he was making for the little work he was doing, it was just too good to walk away from.

He had gone to war to fight for the American dream, and now he was living it.

In his pocket, his cell phone vibrated.

He opened his eyes. Outside the narrow opening of the steel hut the desert stretched out in front of him. The day had worn on and the sun was already headed toward the horizon. In another hour it would be gone. Night would come, and the temperature would drop, and the desert would become alive with the nocturnal sounds of nature. And the sniper? By then he would be home, his feet up on the ottoman, *SportsCenter* on the widescreen.

The audiobook was getting to a good part, the detective close to finding out who the killer was, and part of him wanted to just keep listening, while another part—the rational part, the part that liked money—woke up his iPod to stop the audiobook. He plucked out the earbuds just as he withdrew the phone from his pocket.

A text message was on the screen: RED MUSTANG, FOUR MILES EAST.

The sniper set the iPod and earbuds aside. He climbed to his feet, stretched his arms, his legs, his neck. He stepped over to the mesh case on the ground, bent and opened it up to reveal an XM2010 enhanced sniper rifle.

The XM2010 was a fine machine. The Army had issued it in 2011, so he hadn't had the pleasure of using it during combat, but he thought he got better use out of it now as a civilian.

The rifle weighed twelve pounds and was nearly four feet long, the barrel exactly twenty-four inches.

He hefted it and exited the hut, keeping low as he advanced to the edge of the ridge. From here he had a perfect view of the valley, and the highway that snaked through it. The closest section was almost a straight shot, nearly two miles of state-maintained pavement, and oftentimes drivers put the pedal to the metal, either to try to save an extra minute or to get a rush.

The red Mustang was still three miles away. He could just make out the dot on the horizon. If the car was going too fast—and he had to assume it would be—it made his job harder. But that was why he got paid the big bucks. Nobody ever said it would be easy.

He lowered himself down into his usual spot. He attached the sound suppressor, made sure it was tight and secure, then opened up the tactical rails, locked them in place, and set the rifle down on the ground.

He closed his left eye and with his right eye peered through the scope.

The range on the rifle was 1,300 yards.

From where he was crouched up on the ridge to the place the Mustang would pass was just under 1,000 yards.

More than enough room for him to play with.

In fact, it was almost child's play.

The XM2010 had a five-round detachable box magazine. He attached it now, though he would only need two bullets. All he ever needed were two bullets, .300 Winchester Magnums.

He took a breath, released it. Took another breath, let it out only halfway.

He looked through the scope again.

There was the Mustang, coming right at him.

His finger touched the trigger.

He waited … waited … waited …

A slight squeeze of the trigger, the kick of the rifle, a quick adjustment; another slight squeeze of the trigger, another kick of the rifle, and that was it. His job for the day was done.

2

Nova was doing seventy-five, the needle inching up toward eighty, Guns N' Roses blasting from the speakers, when the Mustang's rear tire blew and nearly sent him careening off the highway.

He only had one hand on the steering wheel—his right—while his left arm was on the open windowsill, his fingers tapping a quiet beat to the pounding music. But once the tire blew and the car began to buckle and he felt the centrifugal force start to pull him off the highway, he grabbed the wheel and gripped it hard, jerking it to the left just a bit, enough to keep him on the macadam.

A second later, the front tire blew—the same side as the rear—and Nova wrestled the wheel again to gain control, then lifted his foot off the gas and coasted to a shaky stop along the side of the highway.

From the speakers, Axl Rose screamed that the jungle was going to bring Nova to his knees.

Nova punched the power on the ancient stereo, cutting Axl off mid-scream.

The engine was still idling, purring like a beast, eager to keep eating up miles.

Nova cut the ignition, withdrew the key, and opened his door.

At once the silence of the desert enveloped him. There were sounds, yes, the desert sounds of nature—wind, cicadas, a bird, possibly a hawk, calling from somewhere nearby—but the sounds he was used to hearing—traffic, construction, people—were absent. It was one of the reasons why he had taken this road trip in the first place, to just get away from it all. But this right here, not one but two of his tires blown flat, had not been part of the plan.

He shut his door—the sound of metal meeting metal becoming the loudest sound in the desert—and circled around the hood to check on the tire.

Yep, the thing was flat, just like the rear tire.

Crouching down, Nova squinted at the worn rubber. The light was leaving the sky, but there was still enough to see that the tire had been shredded in one spot. Even though he knew he was going to find the same thing, he checked the rear tire.

"Son of a bitch."

He stood back up and stared down the empty space of highway he'd just driven. He hadn't noticed anything in his path, broken glass or shaved metal, anything to cause two tires to blow like that … though he had been getting into the song at the time, singing along with the chorus like a jackass.

There was a spare tire in the trunk, but it was just one spare, and right now one spare was not going to help.

He withdrew his iPhone from his pocket, slid the bar across the screen, entered his PIN, but then said, "You've got to be shitting me."

NO SERVICE, the iPhone informed him.

Nova held up the phone, slowly turned himself in a full three-sixty as if that might magically restore cell service.

It didn't.

Nova released a heavy breath. He knew what this meant. He knew what it meant and he didn't like it one bit.

The last town he had passed through was about six miles back. It had been a small town, a handful of houses, trailers, some buildings, and not much else. He wasn't sure how far up the next town was, and without cell reception, he couldn't check Google Maps.

Which meant he had no choice but to head back the way he had come.

He considered grabbing one of his bags from the trunk but decided he only needed his leather jacket instead. The temperature wasn't too bad—was rather comfortable, in fact—but he knew just how cold it got in the desert. In the next hour or so, once the sun disappeared, it would be best to have a jacket.

He locked the doors and stood back from the car for a moment to take in its beauty.

It was a 1966 Mustang Shelby GT 350, cherry red with white racing stripes. He had always wanted a Mustang, ever since he was a kid, and had promised himself he would eventually buy one. But then life, as it always did, got in the way, and he was barely home long enough to enjoy such a car.

But then all that shit went down back in D.C., and his pickup ended up in the Potomac, and then he quit his job and needed a new ride and figured, what the hell, he'd always wanted a Mustang, didn't he?

The price for this one was a pretty penny—just over six figures—but it was more than worth it and Nova had the extra money to spend so he went all out.

And now here it was, a vintage classic with two blown tires, sitting slumped along the side of an empty highway in the Nevada desert.

"Son of a bitch," Nova said again.

He started walking.

3

It took him an hour before he saw the town off in the distance—a few lights in the growing darkness—and it took him another twenty minutes before those lights materialized into actual buildings. By then the sun had set and the temperature had dropped, just as Nova had known it would, and he was doubly glad he had brought along the leather jacket.

For the first mile or so he had focused on the sun-weathered macadam, trying to spot anything that might have caused two of his tires to blow, but besides a flattened can of Old Milwaukee along the side of the highway, there was nothing.

Traffic was sporadic for the most part, the first vehicle passing him a tractor-trailer. It had been coming toward him, away from town. He stuck out his thumb anyway, in the hopes the driver would stop, so Nova could use the CB radio. But the truck had just kept going—the trailer itself white with no markings on its side—and Nova had watched it receding, noting the license plate was from California.

A few other vehicles had passed him along the way—some

headed west, others headed east—but by then he had no interest in hitching a ride. He would reach town soon enough.

He checked his phone every half mile, hoping for a signal. None was available. It was strange—he had been passing through most of rural America in the past two days and there had almost always been cell reception. Granted, it was usually only one or two bars, and even those weren't reliable, but at least they had been something.

Strangely enough, as he neared town—nearly a half mile away—service was suddenly restored to his phone. Four bars, even, more than enough to make a phone call or use the Internet. He unlocked the screen, pulled up the phone application, but then realized he had nobody to call. He wasn't a member of AAA, and even if he was he knew it didn't matter unless there was a tow truck nearby, and if there was a tow truck nearby, then he might as well find it himself. The town looked small enough to walk from one end to the other in five minutes, so he kept walking.

Most of the town—houses and trailers—sat off on one side of the highway. On the other side was a diner and a bar, as well as a long, squat building that he realized after a moment was a motel. Behind the motel sat two dust-covered tractor-trailers.

Nova tried the diner first. The lights were on inside, but the doors were locked. A sign on the door said the diner closed at eight. He checked his watch. It was 8:15.

Inside, a middle-aged woman was wiping down the tables and counters. Another was mopping the linoleum floor. The one wiping tables noticed him, smiled and shrugged.

He went to the motel next. It appeared to have six rooms. There was only one car in the parking lot, a Volkswagen Rabbit convertible.

He couldn't seem to find an office. All there appeared to be were the six rooms, and only one of them—occupied by the owner of the Rabbit, presumably—had lights on inside. He was half-tempted to knock on the door, inquire how one went about contacting the front desk, if such a front desk existed, but decided not to bother.

Nova headed for the bar.

4

Outside the bar were parked three pickup trucks, two beaters, three motorcycles. Judging by the number of vehicles, he assumed there might be a dozen patrons inside at the most, but when he walked through the door he found double that amount, mostly men but a few women, too, sitting at tables and booths. None of them occupied the bar, where Nova headed through a fog of cigarette smoke and country music, instinctively veering toward the corner of the bar, so he could view the room with his back up against the wall.

The bartender was an older woman who had seen better days. She wore too much makeup and her hair had been bleached down to the roots. She barely acknowledged Nova at first, standing behind the bar, puffing on a cigarette, staring into space.

Finally Nova said, "Can I get a drink?"

She blinked and studied him for a long moment, before crushing her cigarette out in an ashtray sprouting used butts. She waltzed over, taking her time, still staring off into space like she would rather be anywhere else but here.

"Whatcha want?"

"Beer."

"What kind of beer?"

"I don't care. Just as long as it's cold."

She pursed her lips, studying him again, before silently grabbing a glass and filling it from one of the taps set up along the bar. Despite the Budweiser and Miller Lite neon signs buzzing in the windows, none of the taps were labeled, so Nova figured it would be a crapshoot to see what he ended up with.

The beer, when she set it down in front of him, had too much head, and the foam overflowed along the sides of the glass.

"Thanks," Nova said. "You got a napkin, too?"

She ignored him. "You want to start a tab?"

"Sure."

The woman started to walk away, probably to grab another cigarette, when Nova said, "Who runs the motel?"

She gave him an irritated look. "What's that?"

"The motel. I'm looking for a room."

"Oh yeah?" She turned to him fully, lighting herself another cigarette. "And why's that?"

"My car broke down a couple miles from here. This time of night, I'm guessing I won't get a hold of a mechanic until morning, so I figured I might as well get a room."

The woman seemed to think about this for a moment before nodding. "You want a room? I can give you a room."

"You manage the motel?"

"The motel, the diner, this bar—I manage it all. One night's stay will cost you eighty bucks."

"Seems pretty steep considering you have six rooms and only one of those is currently being used."

Her eyebrow lifted. "You trying to haggle with me? Because I don't have to rent you a room at all."

"Eighty's fine. Where can I get a key?"

"The keys are already inside the rooms, right on top of the pillows. But don't expect to find any mechanic in the morning."

"Why's that?"

"There ain't any. At least there ain't any around here. The closest mechanic shop is in Townsend, the next town over, and that's at least twelve miles. They'll send someone out, but it might take most of the day."

This wasn't the news Nova wanted to hear, but he wasn't surprised. He had passed through towns just as small as this in the past two days, towns that barely deserved a dot on the map, so he couldn't complain. At least he had a place to lay his head down, even though he was beginning to think the sheets might not have been washed in a while.

Laughter exploded at a booth off in the corner, a trio of beefy men pounding the tabletop.

The bartender started to drift away again, and Nova said to her, "Small town, huh?"

She sighed, turning back to him. "You seen any smaller?"

Nova shrugged and took a sip of the beer. He had expected something watered down, but it wasn't. It was surprisingly good. He held the glass up and squinted at the amber liquid.

"What kind of beer is this?"

"Good beer," the bartender said. "Any other questions?"

"What's the name of this town anyway? I didn't see any signs on the way in."

The bartender flashed nicotine-stained teeth. "Honey, welcome to Parrot Spur."

5

It was another hour before the girl came into the bar.

Nova pegged her as the driver of the VW Rabbit at once. She just didn't have the look of a local. The men and women here, their skin was baked brown by the sun, but this girl was pale, brunette, and looked like she had just stepped out of a college classroom. Even her clothes were incongruous with the rest of the place—jeans and a polo shirt, yes, but they were clean and bright, not faded and worn like the clothes of everyone else in the bar. The only thing that was faded and worn was the Detroit Tigers baseball cap fastened on her head.

She looked around the room for a long moment, as if deciding where to sit, before heading straight for the bar. She took a seat several bar stools away from Nova, who was working on his fourth beer.

He had asked the bartender if there was any food, and she slid a bowl of pretzels in front of him, but the pretzels looked as appealing as a make-out session with the bartender, so he just kept drinking. It took a lot to get Nova drunk, but these four beers had given him a nice buzz. Really, he should have just paid his tab and headed for the motel, picked a room and stripped the bed to make sure there were no creepy crawlies waiting for him under the covers, and then closed his eyes and drifted off to sleep.

And he was going to do that right after he was done with this beer, but then the girl came in—the girl who clearly didn't belong—and Nova decided to wait. He had immediately sensed a shift in the atmosphere the moment she stepped inside. It hadn't been anything overly apparent—the country music hadn't abruptly stopped—but he had noticed the shifting eyes, the leaned-in whispers.

Nova didn't like it, so he decided to wait.

He didn't have to wait long.

The girl had barely ordered a beer before one of the men approached her. He was one of the trio who had been guffawing earlier. Nova watched him as he rose from the booth, hitched his pants, grinned at his friends, grabbed the empty pitcher on the table, then slowly made his way to the bar, wagging his butt drunkenly while his two friends were busting up laughing. The guy made it to the bar, which so far was only occupied by Nova and the girl, and he leaned in right beside the girl, holding a finger up for the bartender's attention.

The bartender placed a beer in front of the girl, took the empty pitcher and placed it under the tap, all the while smoking her cigarette.

Even over the music, Nova could hear the guy ask the girl her name.

The girl, clearly uneasy, forced a smile at him. "Hi."

The guy laughed. "Your name's Hi? Well, shit, I never heard that name before. Hi, Hi." The guy grinned back at his friends, then leaned in closer. "So, Hi, you like fruit?"

The girl took a sip of her beer but said nothing.

"Apples, oranges, bananas?" When the girl still didn't answer, the guy said, "What about cherries? You like cherries, Hi?"

The girl was doing her best to ignore the guy, but that just fueled the fire. The guy grinned back at his friends again, trying not to laugh, before he continued.

"You like the way cherries taste, Hi? I love the way they taste. I love popping them in my mouth every chance I get. Do you like popping cherries, Hi?"

Nova groaned inwardly. It wasn't the guy's asinine one-sided conversation—though, truthfully, it was pretty bad—but the fact that Nova couldn't force himself to sit by passively any further while this girl got harassed.

He pushed his bar stool back with enough force the legs scraped across the floor, and started to make his way down the length of the bar.

"Hey, buddy," he said. "I think you should take your pitcher and go back to your table."

The bartender, who had already filled the pitcher and set it on the bar top, took one last drag of her cigarette before she slowly backed away.

The guy tilted his face toward Nova, studied him for a beat, then snorted. "Get lost, asshole."

Nova took a deep breath as he settled himself down onto the stool beside the guy. "See, with that type of disrespectful attitude, it's no wonder the lady doesn't want to talk to you."

The guy had turned away from Nova, but now he turned back, slowly, as if somehow the slowness with which he turned would increase his intimidation factor.

"The fuck did you just say?"

"Your disrespectful attitude," Nova said. "Believe it or not, women aren't attracted to assholes such as yourself. They might like the bad boy, but a bad boy doesn't also mean asshole. See, there's a difference."

Now the man was turned completely in Nova's direction. The distance between them was only a couple feet. If the guy wanted to throw the first punch, or even the first kick, he would have more than enough room to strike. Assuming, of course, Nova just sat there and let it happen. Which Nova did not intend to do. Not here. Not anywhere. His whole plan had been to draw attention away from the girl, place it on him, but now that he was close to the man, saw just how tall and built the guy was, he realized he might have overplayed his hand. Nova was quite skilled in hand-to-hand combat, and there had been times when he had to fight several men at once, but a gut feeling he'd had the moment he stepped into this bar suddenly confirmed itself, and Nova knew he was outmatched. But that didn't mean he was going to back down.

"Asshole," the guy said, his face turning red, the cords on the sides of his neck sticking out, "you better do yourself a favor and get the fuck out of this bar before I rearrange your face."

Nova held the guy's stare for a beat, just long enough to sense that everyone else in the bar was now watching them. From the corner of his eye he saw that the guy's friends were preparing to join in.

Which meant that, when the guy's two friends joined the fun, it would be three against one. As long as the rest of the bar didn't get into the mix, too.

"Rearrange my face?" Nova smiled, shaking his head. "That threat is about as scary as your breath. Which, I should add, smells like ass. Say, between your two friends over there, whose ass tastes better?"

And the guy's friends were already on their feet by the time the guy threw the first punch.

6

Nova saw the punch coming. After all, he had been expecting it, had been baiting it, and would have been greatly disappointed had it not come.

The guy was right-handed and put everything he had into the punch.

Nova ducked it easily enough, the guy's fist inches from his face, and immediately stepped in and kneed the guy in the balls. As the guy bent forward, Nova grabbed his hair and smashed his head against the bar top.

By then the guy's two friends were already coming at Nova, and Nova turned to meet them, squaring his shoulders, deciding which one to take out first. One had a goatee and a nose which had clearly been broken many times, while the other had a shaved head and tattoos on his arms.

Nova figured Tattoo was the weaker of the two, so as they hurried forward, he stepped toward Goatee.

Goatee feinted a left cross but ended with a right hook instead. It caught Nova off guard, despite the fact he had used a similar ploy countless times in the past. Goatee's fist connected with Nova's jaw, then immediately Goatee went for Nova's solar plexus, hammering it hard.

Nova stepped back, blocked the next blow, leaned in and used his elbow against Goatee's throat. As the man started to go down, Tattoo kicked Nova in the back of the knee. Nova started to stumble, managed to stay on his feet, but by the time he turned Tattoo was there with a quick one-two punch at Nova's face.

Nova stumbled back into a table. Tattoo came at him again, and Nova deflected the next several punches before managing to get in a right hook. It sent Tattoo flying back into another table, tipping it over and sending several beer bottles crashing to the floor.

Other patrons in the bar had risen to their feet, but none looked ready to step in just yet, waiting to see how this played out. From the speakers a country singer sang about his dog and his pickup truck and some girl named Marlene.

Nova turned back to check on the first guy when another punch came directly at his head. He turned his face at the last instant, enough so that the fist didn't shatter his nose, but still blood blossomed everywhere. Nova turned back, meaning to charge the guy, when suddenly he was grabbed from behind in a sleeper hold.

This had to be Goatee. Nova was faintly aware of the scars on the arms holding him in place. He didn't even bother fighting the hold, knowing that would only waste his energy. The arm on his throat tightened, and Nova steeled himself, ready for what came next.

Which, as it turned out, was the first guy, his head bleeding, walking right up to him.

"Told you I'd rearrange your face, didn't I?"

The guy never had a chance. As he raised his fist, Nova leaned back into Goatee and lifted his feet and kicked straight out. His shoes connected with the guy's chest, toppling him over, just as gravity sent Nova and Goatee crashing into another table.

More beer sloshing the ground, more bottles shattering, a faint sense of glass pebbles biting into his arm. As Goatee struggled to his feet, Nova stayed where he was on the dirty floor, just waiting until Goatee stood up fully and turned to him, and then Nova kicked Goatee straight on his shin.

The desired effect was nearly nauseating—the bone snapping, Goatee crying out as he hit the floor—and Nova was back on his feet just as Tattoo charged at him. Nova gave it a second, waiting for the guy, and he used the guy's momentum to grab him and throw him into another table.

He heard a shoe crunch something behind him and immediately ducked another blow, then reached out and grabbed the first guy's throat and swept his legs out from under him, throwing him to the ground, the back of the guy's head bouncing off the dirty floor.

"I told you," Nova said, "nobody likes an asshole," and he raised his fist to smash the guy's face when suddenly a gunshot went off.

All at once everything went still. The country music kept going, but everyone else had stopped moving—had even stopped breathing—for the second or two it took to focus their attention on the door and the old man in a brown police uniform and his sidearm aimed at the ceiling.

He said, "What the hell is going on in here?"

1

The holding cell was tiny, barely the size of a closet, with a cot crammed into half the space and a steel chair set up against the wall.

Nova said, "You expect me to stay in there all night?"

Sheriff Leonard Smith sighed. "Like I told you, you won't be locked in, but if you want a place to sleep tonight, this is your only option. After what you did to Nancy Price's bar, she don't want you in any of the rooms she rents out, and quite frankly, I don't blame her."

"I already offered to pay for the damages."

"Yes you did, and I believe it was much appreciated, but the fact is you beat up three of the local boys and caused quite a ruckus in the process."

"A point of clarification—the one guy swung at me first."

"That he did, and I'm not denying it, but from what I hear you egged him on."

Nova said nothing.

The sheriff sighed again. "Look, like I told you, you're not under arrest. None of those boys are pressing charges, and I believe you're maintaining the position that you don't want to press charges either, isn't that correct?"

Nova, standing with his arms crossed, staring into the pathetic excuse for a holding cell, nodded distantly.

"Still, the fact is, you brutally assaulted one of those boys." The sheriff raised a hand before Nova had a chance to try to dispute the claim. "You did, and you know you did. That boy's leg is split in two thanks to you, and it's not like we have any hospitals around here."

"Yeah, I was wondering about that," Nova said. "You don't really have much around here at all, do you?"

"We have all that we need, and we're thankful for it. As for a hospital, no, the closest one is twenty miles from here, and by now I hope they have poor Lloyd in the emergency room getting the care he needs."

"So what does everyone do?"

"Pardon?"

"This town doesn't have much. From what I can see there's just the bar, the diner, and the motel. What do people do for work?"

"Parrot Spur used to be a mining town, way back when, but the mine closed decades ago. So you're right—this town doesn't have much at all. That's why almost everyone heads into Townsend for work. There's a factory there."

Nova looked around the cramped space that made up the sheriff's office. There was a desk, some folding chairs, a coffee maker, and that was about it. Besides the entrance door there were two other doors, one leading to a bathroom, the other leading to this holding cell.

"Why does this town even need a sheriff?"

So far the older man had been tolerant of Nova, at least as tolerant as a local sheriff can be to a stranger who busted up three local men and destroyed half the bar doing it. He clearly wasn't happy about the situation, but he also clearly understood the circumstances behind it, and he wasn't going to unfairly single Nova out. And Nova, being the doofus that he was, had to go and insult the sheriff with a stupid question.

His face hard, his voice tense, the sheriff said, "Every town needs a sheriff, no matter how small it is. Now are you going to use the cot or not?"

Nova nodded again. "I'll use it. Thanks."

The sheriff turned away and shuffled toward his desk. Pulling a ring of keys from his belt, he picked through them until he found the key he wanted and then used it to lock all the drawers.

Nova asked, "What about my car?"

"What about it?"

"According to Ms. Price, I have to call Townsend in the morning to get a tow."

Nodding absentmindedly as he locked the last drawer, the sheriff said, "That's right, you're gonna call Abbott and Sons. That's the mechanic shop over in Townsend. But despite its name, Ed Abbott doesn't have any sons. It was a family business, his father being the first Abbott. Anyhow, he only has one other mechanic, and judging by how busy they might be with oil changes and whatnot, they might not get to your car until later in the day."

"Fantastic," Nova said dryly. "Considering that the diner is the only game in town for food, you think Ms. Price will allow me in her establishment for breakfast?"

The sheriff headed for the door, replacing the ring of keys on his belt. "Guess we'll see what happens in the morning, won't we?"

8

At seven o'clock the next morning Nova left the sheriff's office just as he had found it. By that time Sheriff Smith—or any of his deputies, if he had any—hadn't shown up yet. Nova didn't feel right leaving the place unlocked, but figured there wasn't much harm in it anyway. As it was, he planned to be right across the highway and could keep an eye on the office until the sheriff arrived ... assuming Nova wasn't kicked out of the diner the moment he stepped inside it.

Besides the two waitresses running orders to tables, the diner had maybe a dozen patrons. Nova recognized half of them from last night at the bar. They recognized Nova, too, but nothing came of it, and Nancy Price didn't appear, so he grabbed a booth in the far back corner with his back against the wall and a view of the entire room.

One of the waitresses brought him a menu. Nova ordered coffee and pancakes and eggs and bacon and waited until the waitress brought his coffee and then he just sat there sipping it. Like the beer from last night, he had figured it would be second-rate, but it tasted strong.

As he waited for his food, he took out his iPhone and noted that the power level was low, almost fifteen percent, and knowing his phone that meant he only had another hour or two before it lost power completely. He opened up the web browser, googled "Townsend, Nevada" and "mechanic" and was promptly given a phone number to Abbott & Sons Mechanic Shop.

He dialed the number, not expecting any answer, but after three rings the phone was picked up and an aged, husky voice said, "Hello?"

Nova explained who he was—well, his alias—and what had happened to his car and how he was currently in Parrot Spur.

The aged, husky voice said, "We can come get your car, but I can't promise an exact time. Maybe in the next hour, maybe in the next five hours. That okay?"

Nova said that was fine. Part of him wanted to reiterate that the car was a vintage classic and how he would prefer the old mechanic get to it as soon as possible, but he knew coming across as an asshole wouldn't be the wisest idea, especially after the events of last night. He thanked the mechanic and disconnected the call just as the waitress brought him his food.

The pancakes were thick and buttery and tasted better than any he'd had in a long time. Even the eggs and bacon were delicious, which surprised Nova, considering that this diner was in the middle of nowhere and probably serviced no more than twenty patrons a day.

It was as he took the last bite of his syrup-drenched pancakes that the girl from last night entered the diner.

Today she wore jeans and a brown T-shirt and sneakers. Like last night, she did a quick survey of the room before continuing forward to find a seat. Nova thought she might choose the counter, but instead she bypassed the counter and strode straight toward him.

Sliding in on the other side of the booth, she said, "I'm not taking anyone's seat, am I?"

Nova shook his head, wiping his mouth with a napkin.

"I didn't think so." She glanced at his empty plate. "Food any good?"

"Surprisingly enough, yes." He set the napkin aside, took another sip of his coffee. "I recommend the pancakes."

"I wouldn't mind trying them, but I doubt they're gluten free."

"You don't like gluten?"

"My mother has Celiac disease, so I've grown up avoiding gluten as much as I can." She smiled. "I'm Jessica, by the way."

"I'm John," Nova said, using his current alias. Even the driver's license and credit cards in his pocket said the same.

"I didn't get a chance to tell you last night, but that was a pretty stupid thing you did."

Nova waited a beat. "You're welcome."

"You don't know me."

"That's true. But that guy was harassing you."

"So? You don't think I could have handled it on my own?"

Nova wasn't quite sure how to answer this. If anything he had been expecting a thank you, not a reprimand. Before he could say anything, though, the waitress appeared with a menu.

"Coffee, hon?"

Jessica nodded and the waitress left and still Nova wasn't sure what to say. Then Jessica, staring back at him, cracked a smile.

"I'm just messing with you," she said. She noticed the bruises on his knuckles, then looked more closely at his face. "Ouch, that really swelled up, didn't it?"

She meant his eye. "It's been better."

"I do appreciate what you did," she said, glancing down at the menu, "but I should let you know I'm not easy."

"I never thought you were. In fact, that was the furthest thing from my mind last night."

"Should I take that as an insult?"

"I just don't like when assholes push their assholeness on others."

"I don't think assholeness is a word."

"How old are you anyway?"

"Twenty-two."

The waitress came back with a coffee. Jessica asked for another minute to look over the menu, and then—the waitress having left them again—asked the obvious question.

"You're not from around here, are you?"

"I was just about to ask you the same thing."

"What brings you out to the middle of nowhere?"

"My car broke down. Two of my tires went flat, about six miles down the highway. I didn't know how much farther the next town was, so I walked back here."

"And ended up in a bar fight." She shook her head like a disappointed kindergarten teacher. All that was missing were the tsks. "You didn't end up getting charged, did you?"

"No, but I'm apparently banned from the bar and the motel. In fact, I'm surprised they let me in this diner."

"Where'd you sleep?"

"Sheriff's office has a holding cell with a cot."

She made a face. "That couldn't have been very comfortable."

"Believe me, it wasn't. So what brings you to the middle of nowhere?"

"Research."

Nova waited a beat, expecting more, and when none was forthcoming, he said, "Research on …"

"I'm a graduate student doing my thesis on mines and their aftereffects." She glanced furtively over her shoulder to make sure nobody was listening and then lowered her voice. "Parrot Spur has a closed mine, so I'm hoping to check it out."

"I don't think they give guided tours."

"No, they don't."

The waitress returned and Jessica, with a sheepish grin,

asked for another minute. The waitress didn't look amused, but she asked Nova if he'd like anything else, and when Nova declined, she tore his check from her pad and placed it facedown on the table.

"When do you plan on trespassing?" Nova asked.

"Sometime later today. Why, you want to tag along?"

"Not really. But as I did you a favor last night, I was thinking maybe you could do me a favor."

"I told you, I'm not easy."

"And I told you, that's the furthest thing from my mind."

"Last night it was. Who knows what's on your mind this morning."

"Anyway," Nova said, "can you do me a favor?"

She smiled. "I guess that depends on what it is."

9

Jessica's VW Rabbit hadn't been constructed with someone like Nova in mind. He was too tall for its cramped passenger side, no matter how far back he adjusted the seat.

"Are you sure this is okay?" Jessica asked, starting the car. "I think I might have some rope in the trunk. We can strap you to the roof if you think that'll be more comfortable."

Nova grinned. "Maybe on the way back."

He had only known Jessica for less than an hour, but he liked her. It wasn't anything sexual, either, though she was a knockout. What it was, really, was she reminded him a lot of Holly Lin with her dry wit and sarcasm and easygoing nature. Thinking of Holly, though, made him think of everything he had walked away from, everything he had lost, and he wondered if not for the hundredth time if she was okay.

Jessica lowered the top and they headed out of town with the wind racing through their hair.

Nova stared through the windshield, expecting to see a dot farther ahead in the next minute or two, but as the miles disappeared beneath them, no dot appeared.

"What's wrong?" Jessica asked.

Nova was looking around the desert, not just the highway itself but the sagebrush and bushes and the smattering of small trees, trying to decide if any of it looked familiar. True, it had been later in the day and the sun was on its way down, casting shadows everywhere, but he had been too pissed off about the car breaking down to really note any of the surroundings. He just knew that it had been about six miles outside of town, and now they had nearly driven that distance, if not more.

"Have you been watching the odometer?"

"Not really."

"We've gone six miles so far, right?"

"At least."

Nova pulled his iPhone from his pocket to see whether or not it had service. It showed three bars.

"Do you want me to pull over somewhere?"

He thought about it for a moment. "No, let's keep going. Maybe the tow truck already came and got it."

But, ten minutes later, after driving another six miles through the desert to Townsend—a much larger town than Parrot Spur, one that certainly deserved a dot on the map—they ended up at Abbott & Sons Mechanic Shop and the old man inside with the name BUD stitched on his shirt shook his head and said nope, they hadn't had a chance to head out yet to pick up the car and what did he say his name was again?

"John," Nova said through gritted teeth, feeling something sour in the pit of his stomach. Part of him wanted to punch a hole through the wall, while another part suggested it might not be beneficial to the wounds already on his knuckles.

"That's right, that's right," the old man said, his aged and husky voice even more pronounced in person. "You called about the Mustang, didn't you?"

"Yes, and we just came from Parrot Spur and it wasn't where I left it along the highway. In fact, it wasn't anywhere."

Beside him, Jessica was quiet. She knew what this meant, just as Nova knew what this meant. Just as Bud, the old mechanic with the aged and husky voice, knew what this meant. The moment Nova had failed to see the Mustang as a dot in the distance, the dry, acrid desert wind buffeting them, that sour feeling had started in his stomach and now it had spread throughout his entire body.

"Oh dear," Bud said quietly. Then his eyes lit up and he forced a smile. "At least you have insurance, don't you?"

10

They found an electronics store sandwiched between a Chinese place and a pizzeria, and this was where Nova purchased a charger for his iPhone. Jessica stayed in the car, and when Nova slid back into the passenger seat, she asked, "Now what?"

"Now we go back to Parrot Spur."

"But your car—aren't you going to call the insurance company? What about the police?"

"Parrot Spur has a sheriff. I can make a report with him."

She maneuvered the Rabbit out of the parking lot and got them back on the road headed toward the highway. "I find it hard to believe that town even has a sheriff."

"Me, too. In fact, I don't understand why the town exists at all. It's barely even a town. Plus …"

He let it trail there, realizing he was thinking out loud, and that what he was about to say next was something Jessica didn't need to hear.

She glanced at him, sunglasses on her face, her dark hair blowing in the wind. "Plus what?"

"Nothing."

"No, tell me."

Nova took a breath, deciding whether or not it was even worth discussing. Then he figured what the hell, he could always use a sounding board.

"I can't say about the entire town, but the men in the bar last night, and the men in the diner this morning? They're all ex-servicemen."

"How do you know?"

"I just do."

"You were in the service, too?"

Nova stared out at the giant factory in the distance, smoke chugging from three narrow stacks. "It doesn't matter what I was."

"What are you now?"

"Between jobs."

"So you're unemployed."

"You could say that."

"Where were you headed?"

"California. Maybe Oregon. Maybe Washington. I don't really know. I was just driving west and figured I'd stop once I couldn't go any farther."

"Why?"

"I wanted to drive across the country."

"But why come through this way? If you're driving through Nevada, wouldn't it make more sense to pass through Las Vegas? There's a hell of a lot more to see in Vegas."

He turned his face away to watch the passing desert. "I don't like Vegas."

"Why not?"

"Bad memories."

Another mile later, neither one having said a word, Nova dug his iPhone out of his pocket and watched the screen.

Jessica asked, "What are you doing?"

"Checking the signal."

"Are you expecting a call?"

"No. But last night, when my car broke down, I had no signal. Even when I started walking back to town, there was no service for the first three miles."

"So, what, it was a dead zone? That's not too hard to believe out here in the middle of nowhere."

"That's what I first thought, too," Nova said, "but so far my phone hasn't lost a signal yet."

They drove for several more minutes in silence.

Nova kept an eye on his phone, while also keeping an eye on the highway in front of them, and at one point he said, "Stop the car."

"What?"

"Stop the car."

Jessica slowed and halted the Rabbit just off the side of the highway. There were two cars behind them that zoomed past without their drivers even giving them a second glance.

Nova got out and started back down the highway. Behind him, he heard Jessica shutting her door and hurrying to catch up with him.

"What is it?" she said. "What's wrong?"

Nova didn't answer. He crossed over to the other side and started walking along the highway headed west toward Townsend. Cicadas trilled in the sagebrush all around them.

"I should have been looking for it the first time."

Jessica kept pace beside him. "Looking for what?"

"That," Nova said, pointing at the flattened Old Milwaukee can on the side of the highway.

A tractor-trailer came up behind them, its driver giving a courteous toot of its horn as it blasted past.

"What about it?" Jessica asked.

"Nothing, really, but I remember seeing it on the walk back last night." Nova kept walking, past the flattened beer can. "It was about two hundred yards or so from where I left the car."

Nova spotted a few streaks of rubber on the macadam, right where he knew they would be, but what he was looking for were tire tracks in the dirt. They went one hundred yards, another one hundred yards, but didn't see anything.

"Maybe you saw a different beer can," Jessica said.

Nova shook his head, staring down at the ground, at the lack of anything substantial in the dirt. Other cars passed them, another tractor-trailer, but Nova ignored them all. He kept his focus on the dirt, knowing that this was where he had pulled off to last night, where he had stopped and left the Mustang after not one but two tires had gone flat. Even from the beginning, on the long walk back into town when he couldn't find anything on the highway, Nova had suspected that something wasn't right, and now he had even more proof. But what any of it meant, he didn't know.

"All right," Nova said finally, when he remembered that he wasn't alone and that Jessica was still there, waiting for him. "Let's head back."

11

If he hadn't needed to take a piss, none of it might have happened.

As it was, the sniper decided to take a break from the audiobook—the killer had just been revealed, the main character's brother-in-law—and he set the earbuds and iPod aside and stood and stretched and headed out of the hut.

The sky was clear and the sun was bright and the temperature was rising. It was these days that he dreaded most. Sure, he had the shade of the hut to keep the angry sun from flaying his skin, but the hut acted as a kind of oven and roasted him alive. He would be covered in sweat some days, and sometimes brought a portable fan to keep him cool.

He started down the embankment toward the hole that he used to relieve himself. He unzipped and did his business, and it was as he was shaking off that he heard the distant blast of a tractor-trailer horn over the ridge.

The sniper tilted his head just slightly, cocking his good ear toward the ridge in case the horn came again.

For several seconds all he heard was the usual wind and the cicadas, nothing else.

He started back toward the hut before veering off toward the short trail leading up to the top of the ridge. The horn just didn't make sense. Not out on this highway, which was fairly traveled but never busy enough to warrant a trucker blasting his horn.

Maybe it was nothing. Maybe it was something. Either way, the horn was going to bug him if he didn't check things out.

As he reached the top of the ridge, he crouched down and inched his way forward. There was a space between two boulders that he sometimes used to peek out through before setting up for a shot, and he used it now to peer down at the highway.

The tractor-trailer was long gone, but the sniper saw why the trucker had briefly sounded his horn. Two people were walking down alongside the highway, a man and a woman, and the man ...

The sniper pulled his spare scope from one of the pockets of his cargo shorts. He glassed the highway and the man and the woman and realized that, yes, the man was the same guy from yesterday, the driver of the Mustang.

Now it appeared the man had made his way back out here with a friend—the girl drove a small white VW—and was looking for ... what, exactly?

The sniper knew there would be no traces of the guy's Mustang. The team that had taken it was completely professional and never left a trace. That didn't mean the guy wouldn't be suspicious. It had happened in the past, but luckily nothing serious had ever come of it. So maybe this was nothing. Maybe—

The sniper squinted, focusing again on the man.

Son of a bitch.

Instead of staying in last night like he had planned, one of his buddies called him up and invited him to the bar, and they had been sitting around a table telling stories and jokes when the man showed up. Which wasn't surprising, seeing as how his car had just broken down and he had nowhere else to go. But then later, after the girl—*that* girl, the sniper realized, the one right there with the small white VW—after she had come in and Wes had gone up to her and started acting like a jackass, this guy had messed up Wes and Tommy and Lloyd— Lloyd who even had to go to the hospital in Partridge. And those three guys were not a trio that could easily be messed with. They were tough dudes. Incredibly tough dudes. And the guy—the guy right now staring down at the dirt where his car had sat less than twenty-four hours ago—had handled them like a pro.

The sniper had seen enough. He crawled backward and stood and replaced the scope in his pocket and brought out his cell phone.

It took two rings before the call was answered.

The sniper said, "We might have a problem."

12

Jessica pulled up in front of the motel and cut the ignition. They just sat there then, listening to the ticking engine, neither one of them speaking.

Finally Jessica said, "So now what?"

Nova shrugged. "Now I thank you for the ride and go on my way." He withdrew a crumpled twenty-dollar bill from his pocket and handed it to her. "Here, for gas."

"Don't worry about it."

"Just take it."

She took the bill from him and said, "But what about your car?"

"Evidently it was stolen. I'll make a report with the sheriff, but I don't expect anything will come of it."

"What are you going to do now?"

"Buy a car, I guess. Not one around here, obviously, but I saw a used car place back in Townsend. I'm sure I can find something reliable for a decent amount."

"You want me to drive you back there?"

"No, you've done more than enough. I'm sure I can hitch a ride. If not, I can always walk."

"It's at least twelve miles."

"I've walked more."

"Don't be crazy. I'll drive you. But we'll have to do it tomorrow."

"That's right," Nova said. "You're trespassing at the mine."

"Trespassing is such an ugly word. Sure you don't want to come with me?"

"As much fun as that sounds, I think I'll pass. But be careful. There's something about this town that doesn't feel right."

"You mean all the ex-servicemen?"

"That and something else. I just can't put a finger on it. Take care of yourself."

He went to open the door when Jessica spoke again.

"Your name really isn't John, is it?"

Nova paused. "Does it matter?"

"I guess not. Just seems odd to go by a fake name."

Nova opened his door and stepped out. "Thanks again."

She restarted the engine, the Rabbit rumbling to life. "Good luck. And remember, if you need a ride tomorrow, I'd be happy to help out."

"I appreciate it," Nova said. He stepped back and watched her reverse out of the space, then pull back onto the highway. He waited until she had passed town completely and became a dot in the distance before heading toward the sheriff's office.

13

The sheriff's office was empty. The door was locked, and when Nova peered through the dust-coated windows, the lights were off inside.

He checked his watch. Not even eleven o'clock in the afternoon yet, and the sheriff and his men—assuming the sheriff had any men—were not there.

Nova considered poking his head back in the bar, but feared that Nancy Price, stationed behind the bar with a cigarette clamped between her cracked lips, would bring up a shotgun and chase him back out. The diner was another option, but judging by the two cars parked out front, the sheriff probably wasn't there either.

Which all put Nova in a particular spot. He could stay here by the sheriff's office and wait in the shade, or he could go and explore the town.

Seeing as how he had always been a restless man, he decided to explore the town.

Of course, that didn't take long at all. Last night Nova had guessed it might take five minutes to walk from one end of town to the other end, and his guess was spot on. He even walked slowly, taking his time, noting the houses and trailers and buildings.

All the buildings were only one story tall. There were thirteen houses, twenty-one trailers (both of the single and double-wide variety), and two buildings, one of which was the empty sheriff's office.

There was no real street that connected these buildings. It was more like a latticework of interconnected driveways. A few had dusty pickups parked in front or beside, while others had dusty motorcycles, a handful had cars.

The buildings were nondescript. Nothing much set them apart from each other. Even the trailers looked the same. One or two had American flags hanging from poles, but that was it. No flowerbeds, no wind chimes, no whirligigs.

Also, it didn't appear as if any of the buildings were currently occupied. Every door and window was closed.

Nova made it to the end of town, which was basically two trailers standing forty yards apart, one of them with a wooden shed beside it, and then just desert until the hills a half mile away. Nothing but chaparral and sagebrush.

He turned, meaning to head back down the drive to the highway, when he noticed tire tracks in the dirt. The drive itself just sort of petered out, but a set of tire tracks originated from the wooden shed and continued out into the desert, into what he now noticed was a sort of beaten path toward the hills. He was half-tempted to continue forward to see where those tire tracks led, but behind him came the approaching low purr of an engine and tires crunching the dirt.

Nova turned and watched a black Crown Victoria slowly drive toward him. He held his ground and waited until it stopped right in front of him—the front bumper less than a yard from his legs.

The driver's side window lowered, and Sheriff Leonard Smith said, "You exhausted from your tour of our small town?"

Nova smiled. "Are you also the tour guide?"

The sheriff laughed. "I could be, but there ain't much to see. Why don't you get in and cool off? I have the A/C on."

Nova circled around the front of the car to the other side. As he slid into the passenger seat, he realized there wasn't much to set it apart as a police car. He wasn't expecting bells and whistles, but there didn't appear to be *anything* that marked it as a cop car. Not even a computer attached to the dashboard. It was, for lack of a better word, just a car.

"Sorry to hear about your Mustang," the sheriff said, as he began to turn the car around and point them back toward the highway.

Nova played it cool. "What do you mean?"

"I called Bud Jasper—he works for Ed Abbott—to give him a heads-up you might be contacting him. He said you already had, that you had even showed up at his place, but that your car … well, shit. I certainly hope you have good insurance."

That was the second person who had mentioned having good insurance.

The sheriff said, "How'd you end up there, anyway?"

"What's that?"

"You were in Townsend this morning and now you're here. That's quite a distance for a man without a car."

"I hitched a ride."

They pulled out onto the highway, passing the empty sheriff's office, passing the bar and diner and motel.

"Where are we headed?" Nova asked.

"Townsend."

"Why?"

The old sheriff gave him a funny look. "Well, why not? There ain't much to do in our town, especially after you're no longer welcome in the bar. But Townsend has restaurants and motels and even a two-screen movie theater if watching movies is your thing."

"My car was stolen."

The sheriff nodded. "And I'm awfully sorry to hear it."

"I'm not really in the mood to watch movies."

"Of course not. But there are a few car dealerships there, too. One used car place has some good deals. They'll get you fixed up in no time."

"You should write up a report about my car."

"And I'll do just that when we get to Townsend."

"Why can't you do it back in Parrot Spur?"

"I could, certainly, but then what? You want to hang out in my office? You want to sleep again on that cot? This would be a whole other matter if that unpleasantness hadn't taken place last night, but as it is, there ain't much for you in Parrot Spur right now. In Townsend they haven't kicked you out of any bars." He grinned at Nova. "At least not yet."

14

Jessica passed the entrance leading back to the mine—it was a simple dirt road, barely noticeable unless you were looking for it—and kept going down the highway for another mile. She drove less than half the speed limit, keeping an eye on the rearview mirror for approaching cars while at the same time trying to spot any other dirt roads. There didn't appear to be any. Jessica wasn't surprised. She had already checked via Google Maps, but that didn't mean something hadn't been created since those satellite images had been taken.

Eventually she passed a place just off the highway that looked perfect. It was nearly two miles away from the dirt road, but it would have to do.

She checked the rearview mirror once again to confirm that there were no cars coming. Up ahead, the highway was long and empty and shimmering in the unforgiving sun.

Jessica stopped the Rabbit along the side of the highway. She backed up just slightly, turned the wheel, and then drove forward off the asphalt into the dirt. The little four-cylinder engine didn't sound happy about being forced to go off-roading, but it managed, and soon Jessica parked behind a copse of sagebrush and trees. It wasn't the greatest hiding place, but it wouldn't be easily seen from the highway, and that was the point.

She grabbed her backpack from the trunk. She opened it to check her supplies: bottles of water, binoculars, camera, and, most importantly, a stainless steel Smith & Wesson .38 Special with a black rubber grip. The cylinder was empty, and with shaking hands she began to load it like she had been shown years ago, one bullet after another, until the whole thing was loaded and she spun the cylinder shut.

Jessica started to put the gun back into the bag, paused, decided that no, she should keep it out.

She tied her hair back into a ponytail, took the Tigers baseball cap from the backseat and fastened it snug on her head. It had once belonged to her brother, the color faded, the bill nicely curved. He had worn it countless times until he had left for the Army, and Jessica, then still in high school, had worn it out of remembrance to him, knowing it was only temporary and that he would want it back when he returned.

She carefully and gently slid the .38 into the waistband of her jeans. She dug into her pocket, slid out her cell phone. She brought up the map application, waited for the GPS to find her location, and then started walking, away from the highway, toward the mine.

15

Sheriff Leonard Smith dropped Nova off at a used car place just inside Townsend, the same one Nova had seen on his previous visit. There weren't any rental places in town, the sheriff acknowledged with a heavy sigh, but he was certain Nova could find something reasonably priced.

"In fact," the sheriff said, "let me talk to the owner and explain the situation. He's a good guy. He'll understand, and won't try to take advantage of you."

He winked when he said this, trying to be a friend, a confidant, a co-conspirator, but Nova simply said, "I appreciate it, but don't put yourself out."

"Trust me, it's no problem."

"Trust me," Nova said, forcing a smile, "a report is all you need to do."

The sheriff didn't look happy about it, but he went about writing up a brief report. He tore off a copy and handed it to Nova, said again how he hoped Nova had good insurance, and then wished him good luck.

Nova stood on the used car lot and watched the unmarked

Crown Vic pull back out onto the highway and head east, toward Parrot Spur, the place Nova was apparently no longer welcome.

Behind him, a middle-aged, rotund man with a tie hanging loose around his shirt collar stepped out of the building and called, "Help you with anything?"

Nova waved him off. "Thanks, but I'm just looking."

"Well"—the man hitched up his pants—"if you need anything, I'll be cooling myself off inside."

Nova didn't even wait for the man to amble away. He started walking, between the parked cars, onto the sidewalk, and then farther into town. And as he walked, he thought about several different things, namely the town of Parrot Spur.

It didn't quite make sense, but a lot of what had been happening lately didn't make sense. Nova had no issues with tiny towns that were barely towns, but at least those towns followed a kind of competent structure. They had families there, children, junk in their front yards if they had front yards at all. They weren't mostly filled with ex-military men. They didn't have a sheriff who didn't drive an actual sheriff's cruiser and only had a desk and computer and coffee machine in his office. They also didn't run you out of town for no good reason.

Pretty soon he came to a diner. It looked a whole lot busier than the one at which he'd eaten breakfast this morning, but for some reason he had the feeling that the food here wouldn't even stack up against what was served back in Parrot Spur.

He checked his watch. It was almost noon. He had another seven hours before it would begin to get dark. He didn't want to waste any time.

Wait—*waste any time*? Just what the hell was that? That line of thinking was the type Holly Lin was apt to do, the type that created trouble. And Nova had walked away from all of that. As far as he was concerned, life should now be trouble-free, worry-free, and stress-free.

The air conditioning in the diner was a pleasant contradiction to the scorching heat outside. He found a booth near the back that overlooked the room. A waitress came to his table, a younger and prettier waitress than the one who had waited on him this morning. She even went so far as to introduce herself—"My name's Megan," she said, as if her name tag wasn't sufficient—and asked Nova how he was doing this fine afternoon. Nova, who normally relished flirting with women, just smiled, said hello, and ordered a cheeseburger and fries. Megan then asked if he wanted a milkshake with that because they made one of the best milkshakes around. Sure, Nova said, sounds great, but when the food arrived minutes later he found the milkshake subpar, the hamburger undercooked, and the fries cold. When Megan checked to see if there was anything else she could get him, he asked what was really on his mind.

"What do you know about the factory?"

"What do you mean?"

"Who works there?"

She started to frown. "I don't think I'm following."

Don't, he thought. Don't do it.

"How many people from Parrot Spur work at the factory?"

The frown stayed in place, but she shook her head. "None. Mostly only people from Townsend work at the factory. Some even from Kadrey. But not Parrot Spur. Nobody from Parrot Spur works anywhere in Townsend."

"So then what do they do?"

She shrugged. "Beats me. Is there anything else I can get you?"

Now it was Nova who shook his head. He stared off into space, telling himself to forget it, to just buy one of the cheap used cars and continue on his way. Whatever secrets Parrot Spur held, they were none of his business. If Holly Lin were here, she would want to find out what those secrets were. That was just what she did. It was in her nature to be curious about things that would inevitably get her in trouble. But she wasn't here, Nova was, and Nova was sensible and reasonable and didn't want to start any more trouble than was necessary.

Megan tore off the check, placed it on the table, smiled and told him to have a great day. Then she started away, taking only a few steps, before Nova called her back. The smile again, a slight flare of hope in her eyes, the young girl maybe thinking Nova was about to ask her for her number.

Instead he asked, "Can you point me in the direction of the hardware store?"

16

She smelled the mine before she saw it.

A faint scent on the wind, that's all it was, so faint it could barely be called anything but a phantom, and yet Jessica knew what that scent belonged to, where it originated, what it was. That was why she was out here, after all, trudging through the desert, her poor four-cylinder Rabbit behind her, the sky blue and cloudless above her. There were other scents around her, too, those of the desert and sagebrush, but it was that underlying scent that excited her most, because it confirmed everything she knew to be true.

This part of the desert was mostly bare, dotted with bushes and trees. She tried to stay inconspicuous as she continued on, noting the occasional distant traffic and hoping nobody noticed her.

Sweat beaded her brow, dripping into her eyes, into her mouth. She tasted salt. She spit it out and took a swallow from one of her water bottles, but just as quickly more sweat got into her mouth and she spit it out again.

The closer Jessica got to the mine, the more aware she became of the gun digging into her lower back. She had held the gun in her hands less than an hour ago, had even held it earlier this morning in her motel room, both times telling herself she could do this. But now, with potential danger so close, could she continue? If anything, now was the time to stop. Now was the time to turn back around and return to her car and drive away, never to look back.

But no, she couldn't do that. She needed to soldier on. You soldiered on when you had no other choice. And Jessica had no other choice. She was risking everything to be here right now. After all the inquiring, after all the investigating, after narrowing down this location, she was risking it all for ... what, exactly? Proof. That's what she was risking it for. Proof. But then what? Once she had her proof, what would happen then? She would call everyone, that's what—the police, the feds, the news media. It wouldn't bring her brother back, but it would be a start to help heal the wound of losing him.

It had been a risk last night going to the bar—a huge risk—but she had wanted to get a sense of the townspeople, and seeing how the diner had been pretty empty when she had dinner, the bar seemed like the best choice. And she had known, almost instantly, that she was in the right place. It wasn't that the bar was filled with men, but that they had been servicemen, either active or retired, it didn't matter, because what bar in the middle of nowhere, especially one over three hundred miles away from the nearest military base, hosted such a mishmash of servicemen? None that Jessica could think of, at least none that existed in the real world, and Parrot Spur was certainly not in the real world.

And then there was John, or whatever his real name was. His car had broken down—two blown tires, the way he explained it—and now his car was gone, stolen, never to be seen again. She felt bad for him, especially after he had helped her last night, taking on three guys at the same time. That's why she sat with him at the diner this morning, and why she was willing to drive him to Townsend to check on his car. He was strong and smart and handsome—okay, gorgeous—and Jessica worried she may have come on too strong. Because this certainly wasn't the time and place, that was for sure, and she knew better. Her question of whether he would like to come along was more out of precaution than anything else, because where she was headed could potentially be dangerous, and last night John proved he didn't have much fear of danger. Still, maybe she should have pressed the issue, did everything she could do get him to come along.

Jessica shook her head, wiping the sweat from her eyes. The ground had begun to steepen. One hundred yards ahead of her the earth just dropped away.

She crouched down and continued forward. Slower now. Quieter. The gun dug into her lower back again, but she no longer considered turning back around. Absolutely not. She was here, and she was going to see this through.

17

The Parrot Spur Mine had been closed for nearly thirty years. The land on which the mine sat was privately owned, though no matter how much research Jessica had done, she couldn't find who actually owned it. As far as anyone was concerned, the mine was closed and abandoned. Yet despite this, a half dozen pickup trucks and SUVs were now parked around the mine entrance.

The entrance was simply a hole cut into the base of a mountain. Thick square slabs of lumber acted as the doorframe, ensuring the entrance didn't fall in on itself. It stood maybe fifty yards away from the pickups and SUVs.

The whole area was a sort of bowl in the earth, completely secluded from the highway just over a mile away. The dirt road went down an incline toward what Jessica immediately thought of as the parking lot. It was a flat space, several hundred yards wide.

Currently nothing moved down in the bowl. The vehicles all stood motionless. A large wooden shed built near the vehicles appeared empty. The wind rustled the sagebrush and scattered dust. A hawk or some other bird of prey cried out in the distance. An occasional tractor-trailer passed by out on the highway. Besides that, the area was silent.

From her research she knew there was another entrance to the mine, a minor entrance that had been constructed decades ago when the mine was active as an escape in the possibility of a cave in. She didn't know where the minor entrance was located, or whether it even existed anymore. Part of her considered trying to find it, but she knew it didn't matter. From this vantage point—crouched behind some rocks—she could hopefully obtain all the evidence she had come here for.

Jessica set down the binoculars. She wiped more sweat from her eyes. She drained the bottle of water, thankful she had brought two bottles but wondering if it would have been best to bring three or four. The sun was scorching, beating down on her. The gun dug into her back again, and she pulled it from her waistband, set it aside. She lowered the bill of her baseball cap, settled back against a rock, and waited.

Another hour passed before she heard voices.

By that point Jessica had begun to burn. She had applied suntan lotion this morning—SPF 40—but in her nervous haste she had left it on the bathroom counter at the motel. Since then the lotion had worn off while the sun continued to do its worst. It didn't help that she was already fair-skinned. She would pay for it later—an unfortunate Spring Break down in the Bahamas taught her that lesson—but she knew it would be worth it. She just had to tough it out, knowing the risk was worth the cost.

She checked her watch and saw that no, not one hour had passed, but two. Or was it three? It didn't matter. What mattered now was that there were voices coming from down in the bowl, several voices, and with those voices there would be—fingers crossed—the evidence she needed.

She dug in her pack for the camera: a Nokia D3000 with a zoom lens. She turned the camera on, then crawled forward and peeked through the rocks.

There were four men down in the bowl. They were loading up two of the SUVs with large black bags. The bags—what looked from this distance like duffel bags—sat on two wagons. She hadn't seen those wagons earlier, so the men must have brought them out of the mine. The men chatted as they loaded up the SUVs, as if this was their every day job. One of them said something loudly, and the rest of them laughed.

Jessica's finger depressed the button on the camera, and the shutter clicked, which worried her at first, because in the silence it sounded loud and she wasn't sure how it sounded down in the bowl. At least none of the men reacted, so she knew she was okay for now.

But still … she would need more. These pictures didn't prove much. They just showed men loading large duffel bags into two separate SUVs. Those bags could contain anything. As long as she couldn't digitally capture what was in those bags, the pictures would be useless.

She needed to go inside the mine. It was crazy, of course, but that's what needed to be done. How else was she going to prove it to the police and feds and DEA and whoever else would care? She needed proof—solid, substantial proof—and a few random pictures wouldn't prove anything. She would have to wait until nightfall, until all the men inside the mine got into their vehicles and headed back to town. She would have to climb down into the bowl, enter that hole in the ground, and find out just what there was inside the mine. She dreaded the idea but it was what she needed to do. Then she would have her proof. Then she could finally get the ball rolling.

She didn't know when it had happened—her mind on other matters—but the men had quieted. One of them was turned in her direction, the three others with their backs to her. The man appeared to be whispering something.

Jessica peered back through the camera. She adjusted the lens. She focused on the man … who was looking directly at her.

Jessica flinched. She went completely still, her entire body trembling.

There was no way that man could see her. Not from where she was hidden. It just had to be her imagination. That was all. Right?

She adjusted the lens again, as far as it would go, trying to focus right on the man's face. He was still whispering to the three other men, yes, but his eyes kept shifting up toward her. Did he really see her, or was it just a coincidence?

It was then Jessica realized the current placement of the sun. Past midday, the sky clear, the sun starting toward the horizon. And Jessica, from where she was crouched, was positioned so the sun was slightly ahead of her. Which meant—

The reflection. The man could see the sun reflecting off the camera lens.

Oh shit.

Jessica didn't want to make any sudden movements, in case the man down there really was watching her, but she didn't want to stay stationary either. So she began to move, slowly at first, backing away from the rocks. When she was certain she was out of view, she scrambled to her feet and hurried to the backpack.

Shoving the camera into the bag, then shoving in the binoculars, she heard the wind and the cicadas and the distant, sporadic traffic out on the highway, but nothing else.

Jessica paused, holding her breath. Blood pounded in her ears. She tried to listen past it, past the wind, past the cicadas, past the distant traffic into the bowl behind her.

Nothing.

Maybe she had been mistaken. Maybe she was just being paranoid.

Slowly, so very slowly, she turned and lowered herself to her knees again and crawled forward, as quietly as she could, until she reached the spot she had been crouched in just a few moments ago.

She took a deep breath, braced herself, and peeked around the rock.

The men were still down there, but they were no longer loading the SUVs. Now they were hurrying across the dirt parking lot, guns in their hands, coming her way.

18

Jessica had run track in high school. She had tried other sports, but track was the one she enjoyed most. It was also the one she excelled at, because she was fast when she wanted to be. Her long, lithe legs made her unstoppable. It had been a few years since she last ran track, and while she jogged every chance she got, she now hoped her speed hadn't left her.

She ran as fast as she could. The backpack slung over her shoulder, bouncing against her back, the wind rushing at her face, she had gone maybe two hundred yards before she realized she had left the gun behind.

Jessica stopped hard, digging her heels into the dirt. She glanced back over her shoulder. She had once run the 200-meter dash in just under twenty-four seconds. The distance now between her and the gun was about that. She could make it there and back in less than fifty seconds.

But who was she fooling? Even if she had the gun in her possession, it wasn't like it would change much. There were four men coming after her—four men with guns of their own—and what was a silly .38 going to do to stop them? She'd be lucky if she got off a few rounds that actually came close to hitting a target, let alone killing one of them. Even the thought of taking one of their lives chilled her, and she knew that, no, she wasn't going to bother with the gun, not now, not ever.

She kept running. Away from the mine, toward the highway. She could see her car in the distance, hidden behind that small copse of trees. That was how flat the terrain was. Just right for someone of her athletic build and prowess. The men chasing her had once been in the Army, had been trained soldiers, but she doubted they still trained. Even if they did, she had a good head start on them.

It was only a few seconds later when the ground off to her right coughed up dirt. The gunshot echoed through the desert an instant later.

Jessica glanced over her shoulder.

The men had already reached the top of the ridge. One of the men had his gun out. He was the one who had just fired. Jessica was pretty sure that if the man had wanted to, the back of her head would now have a bullet in it. So this man had spared her life, though she knew it wasn't because of any altruistic reason. It had been a warning shot, that was all, a warning shot to show her just what he could do if he wanted to.

Jessica kept running.

She expected another gunshot and wasn't surprised when the ground off to her left again spat dirt. Another warning shot. She wasn't going to get lucky with a third.

She started weaving, trying to make herself a harder target, trying to make her direction as unpredictable as possible. It was the only thing she could do right now to avoid the inevitable. She had even started crying, tears in her eyes now mingled with sweat, knowing that at any second she might die.

Then, suddenly, the earth disappeared beneath her. The next thing she knew she was on the ground, her ankle burning with pain. She tried standing back up, tried pushing herself to her feet, but the pressure on her ankle was too much.

No, she thought or said or cried, no please no please no.

She looked back over her shoulder. More tears were in her eyes, and she blinked them away, saw the men heading toward her. They were fanned out, all with guns in their hands. They weren't running. They were taking their time. Like a group of cats playing with an injured mouse right before they made the kill.

Jessica started crawling. She saw the highway off in the distance, a tractor-trailer headed west. She screamed for help, screamed until her throat went raw, but none of it mattered. Nobody could hear her but the men behind her.

The men, she realized, the thought making her blood run cold, that were now laughing as they made their slow, steady advance.

19

The trucker didn't give his name, and as far as Nova was concerned, that was just fine by him. The man didn't seem like a friendly type—he had been more than irritated when Nova first approached him back at the gas station—and his social skills were poor, but he was headed west, back toward Parrot Spur, and twenty bucks was getting Nova a lift into town. After all, it was less than a fifteen-mile ride, and the trucker was already headed in that direction, so why not?

Company regulations, that was why not, the trucker had told Nova. But then he paused, seemed to reconsider, and sighed saying what the hell, hop in.

And so Nova was in the truck's cabin, staring out the open passenger-side window, the wind breezing through his hair. It made him think about being in the convertible only a few short hours ago, and he wondered how Jessica was faring on her own mission.

As the highway curved and the desert opened up, Parrot Spur could be seen about a mile away, just a cluster of buildings in the middle of nowhere.

Nova checked the side mirror, saw no cars behind them, and said, "You can drop me off here."

The trucker gave him a brief, blank look. "Say again?"

"You can drop me off along here."

"But you paid me to drop you off in town. I told you, it was against company regulations, but I figured what the hell, I can make an easy twenty bucks, and the deal was to drop you off in town so I'm gonna drop you off in town."

"Here's another twenty," Nova said, pulling a bill from his pocket and holding it out toward the trucker.

The trucker went to snatch the bill, but Nova pulled it back. "Only if you drop me off now," he said.

The trucker looked even more irritated than before, but his eyes stayed on the twenty-dollar bill a moment too long. Finally he grunted, checked his side mirror, then downshifted.

"Thank you," Nova said. He extended the bill again, and this time didn't pull it away when the trucker went to snatch it.

"Whatever," the trucker mumbled as he halted the tractor-trailer long enough for Nova to jump down from the cab and slam the door shut. Then, almost immediately, the rig was moving again, the engine groaning as the trucker shifted gears. Nova stood on the side of the highway, the canvas bag strapped over his shoulder, watching the tractor-trailer go. He waited several moments, made sure nobody was coming in either direction, and then hurried across the highway.

The pickings at the hardware store hadn't been as plentiful as Nova would have liked. In the end he had purchased binoculars, rope, a utility knife, and an air-powered nail gun, a full battery pack and gas canister included. The nail gun was because he currently didn't have a gun of his own. Whether he would need a gun was still debatable, but he didn't want to be completely defenseless on the off chance he would need protection.

He had also purchased a canvas bag which contained all of these new items, along with his leather jacket which he had balled up and stuffed inside.

He kept low as he moved through the desert. He was approaching the town at an angle which would take him toward the back of the houses and trailers. The tracks he had seen in the dirt originating from that wooden shed kept bugging him. Those tracks had belonged to a dirt bike, and that dirt bike had been leading toward the hills, away from the direction of the mine. It could have been nothing—maybe one of the townspeople just liked to dirt bike for fun—but he had seen the slight hesitation in Sheriff Smith's eyes when he pulled up and saw what Nova had noticed, and it was that slight hesitation that sparked Nova's curiosity.

At one point he stopped and pulled the binoculars from his bag and looked to see if anything was happening in town. Unsurprisingly, the place looked deserted. There were a few cars parked out in front of the diner and bar, but that was it. Jessica's Rabbit was nowhere to be seen.

He continued on, taking his time, wanting to make sure he was as inconspicuous as possible. He knew he didn't have to go the entire way to town. He remembered where the dirt bike trail had led, and it was in that direction he eventually steered himself.

When he found the trail, he paused for a moment, realizing that he had brought along binoculars and rope and a knife and a nail gun—a fucking *nail* gun, what was he thinking?—but he had failed to bring any water.

Perfect.

Nova could beat himself up about it later. As it was, the day was wearing on and he didn't want to get caught too far out in the desert by the time the sun set. He told himself he would spend only a half hour more on this, maybe an hour, and that was it. As far as he knew, this was nothing.

Still, he told himself, it was a lead, and right now he didn't have anything else to do.

Nova trudged onward.

It didn't take him a half hour before he found the dirt bike. It barely even took him twenty minutes. Without needing to weave in and out of the smattering of sagebrush and trees, he made good time. True, the ground eventually did begin to rise up over the hill, and things got stickier there, but he managed it and then kept going, following the trail which seemed to follow the ridge.

And then he found the dirt bike.

It just sat in the shade of a small scrub tree, propped up by its kickstand, all by itself. Its rider was nowhere to be seen.

Nova looked around the area. Suddenly he felt exposed. What if he was being watched?

The ground here wasn't covered in as much packed dirt, so the tracks weren't as obvious as they had been back in town, but Nova saw the boot prints leading away from the dirt bike. They headed up the hill toward the ridge, past rocks and boulders and more sagebrush.

Nova surveyed the hill, trying to spot another way to ascend that wasn't directly following the boot prints. There didn't appear to be any.

He released a long, heavy sigh. "What the hell am I doing?" he muttered.

When no answer came, Nova started up the hill.

20

The sniper enjoyed variety with his lunches. Yesterday was tuna fish and barbecue potato chips and soda. Today he had packed a turkey BLT, sour cream and onion potato chips, and iced tea.

He was enjoying his lunch now, sitting in the shade of the steel hut, both of the battery-controlled fans cooling him off while he crunched on the last couple of chips. He crumpled up the bag and tossed it in the cooler. He stood then, stretching his legs, swirling the dregs of his drink around the bottle before taking one last swallow. He deposited the bottle in the cooler and ducked his head as he stepped outside the hut.

The sun was stark and brutal, the air dry, and the sniper couldn't wait to call it a day.

"Howdy," said a man standing several feet away, the man from the bar last night, the Mustang's owner. The man nodded his head at the hut. "Nice digs you got there."

The man wore jeans and a gray T-shirt. A canvas bag hung off a strap across his chest. In the man's hand was an air-compressed nail gun. He held it at his side, not aimed at the sniper, but clearly making it known that it could be aimed within the matter of a second.

"Yeah, about that," the man said, gesturing with the nail gun, "it doesn't look pretty, and it's heavier than I would prefer, but it does the trick."

To demonstrate, the man tilted the nail gun and squeezed the trigger and a nail embedded itself in the ground a couple inches from the sniper's feet.

"Not quite a bullet, but I'm sure it stings. Now why don't you turn around, get down on your knees, and place your hands on the back of your head."

The sniper said nothing. He didn't move.

The man gestured again with the nail gun. "Are you really going to make me shoot you with this thing?"

Still the sniper said nothing.

"What are you doing out here, anyway?"

The sniper said nothing. He was too busy thinking. Too busy assessing the situation and his surroundings and deciding just what his options were. Besides the nail gun, there was a canvas bag slung across the man's chest, and there was no telling what other goodies were stored inside. And the man, the sniper knew, was more than just a regular guy—he was a pro, ex-military without a doubt, and after seeing what the man was capable of last night, the sniper didn't want to give the man any more advantage than he already had.

"Well?" the man said.

The sniper thought about it for another moment. He could try to duck back inside the hut, scramble for the XM2010, but the rifle wasn't loaded. Even if it was, it wouldn't matter anyway. The moment he turned away, the man would shoot him with the nail gun. Not that a nail would kill him, but it would certainly slow him down, and who was to say how many times the man might keep shooting?

Gritting his teeth, the sniper raised his hands and turned

around. He lowered himself first to one knee, then the other, but kept his hands up at his sides.

"Place your hands on the back of your head," the man said. "Come on, you know the drill. Thread them together."

The sniper did so, slowly, his eyes shifting down to the ground around him. Sweat was beginning to bead on his forehead. As the man began to make his approach, the sound of his shoes on the dirt slow and steady, the sniper knew that the man would have to put down the nail gun if he intended on binding the sniper's wrists together. Which was exactly what the man started to do—the space between them less than five feet—and as soon as the sniper heard the man pull something from the canvas bag, he made his move.

Grabbing fistfuls of dirt, then standing and spinning, he threw the dirt at the man's face—the man who hadn't put down the nail gun, after all, but still had it in his right hand. It all happened in less than a second, but even in that second it gave the man enough time to fire off a nail.

The nail dug deep into the sniper's shoulder but he didn't let it slow him, advancing on the man who was turning away, coughing, reaching for his eyes. The sniper kicked the man in the back of the knees, sending him to the ground, then grabbed the nail gun the man had dropped and aimed it at the man's face.

The sniper pulled the trigger but the man was already leaning back, out of the nail's way, and then jumping quickly to his feet, swinging a fist at the sniper's face. The sniper saw it coming but only managed to turn away just slightly, enough that the man's fist met the tip of his jaw. He tried to bring the nail gun back up but it was swatted out of his hand, and the next thing he knew he felt an elbow in his stomach. The sniper managed to block the next blow and threw a fist of his own, and for the next several seconds that's all it was, a flurry of fists and kicks and elbows, the man finding a weak spot, then the sniper finding a weak spot, neither one speaking as they parried, until suddenly one tripped the other and they were on the ground, rolling around on the dirt, one's hand on the other's throat, then one's fist digging into the other's stomach, and the nail in the sniper's shoulder was completely forgotten until the man, straddling him on the ground, grabbed a nearby rock and used it to hammer the nail even deeper into the sniper's shoulder.

The sniper groaned in pain. He tried to push the man off him but the man used the same rock against the side of the sniper's head. It didn't knock the sniper out, but it certainly caused him to lose focus. The next thing he knew he was flipped over and his hands were being pulled behind his back. He felt plastic touch his skin and tighten, binding his wrists together, and then the pressure decreased as the man stepped away.

"So"—the man clapped the dust from his hands, clearing his throat—"did that nail sting or what?"

21

Rick took one last drag on his cigarette, tossed it away, and said, "How much longer?"

Mike glanced at his watch. "I dunno. Another hour, maybe two. He said he'd get here as soon as possible."

"Yeah, but he's, where, down in Vegas?"

Mike shrugged. "He didn't say where he was. Just that he'd be here as soon as possible. You might want to make sure you clean up those butts before he gets here, you know what's good for you."

"Yeah, yeah," Rick said, lighting himself another cigarette.

Mike's phone buzzed. He pulled it from his pocket, said, "It's Dan," and placed the phone to his hear. "Go ahead."

He listened for several long seconds, nodding, saying, "Uh-huh, uh-huh," then saying, "Okay, sounds good," before slipping the phone back in his pocket.

Rick said, "What's up?"

"They didn't find anything at the motel. Not even an ID."

Rick nodded, taking another long drag on his cigarette. He glanced over at the girl sitting on the ground against his truck.

Her ankles were bound, her wrists tied behind her back. A piece of duct tape was over her mouth, though Rick wasn't sure why, as the girl had refused to say a word since they found her. Yeah, she had screamed for help at first, but once it was clear no help was coming, she quieted up real fast. Almost too fast. Even when they threatened her, she wouldn't speak. Pete had the bright idea of notifying Sam, who then called Connelly, who said he would be there as soon as possible and not to touch the girl until he arrived. Now they were waiting just outside the mine, Rick and Mike and the girl, while Dan and Pete had already searched the girl's car and now her motel room and found nothing, while the eggheads worked inside the mine without a clue of what was happening out here.

Mike snapped his fingers suddenly. "Shit, I just thought of something."

Rick blew smoke out of the side of his mouth. "What's that?"

"You should text Joe and let him know what's going on. Maybe have him head over here."

Rick didn't move at first, smoking his cigarette, but when Mike kept watching him, he withdrew his phone from his pocket and typed a quick text. Why Mike didn't just do it himself, Rick didn't know, but he didn't feel like arguing. He was as irritated as anyone else. They should be an hour away by now, driving the product to the drop-off point. Instead they were stuck here at the mine, babysitting.

He finished his cigarette and flicked the butt to the ground.

"Seriously," Mike said, "you better make sure you clean those up before he gets here."

"Yeah, yeah," Rick said, and placed another cigarette between his lips.

22

The cooler was well stocked, or had been well stocked earlier in the day. Now there were two bottles of water and a 32oz Gatorade.

"Cool Blue?" Nova said, extracting the bottle of Gatorade from the cooler. "Seriously?"

The man said nothing.

Nova shook the bottle and cracked the top and took a sip. He looked at the bottle again, tilting his head back and forth as he smacked his lips. "Not bad, I guess."

The man still said nothing. He just sat there on the ground, his hands bound behind his back, his ankles bound together, glaring up at Nova.

"So what's the XM2010 for?" Nova asked.

The man said nothing.

Nova sat on a large rock across from the man and took a long swallow of the Gatorade. "We can sit here all day if you want. I've got nowhere else to go."

The man said nothing.

Nova had already searched him. Besides a set of keys—one

of which belonged to the dirt bike, Nova figured—was a cell phone. The cell phone was locked, and Nova knew better than to ask the man for the passcode.

"Parrot Spur is an interesting town. I've never seen so many ex-military in one place outside an Army base. Your sheriff told me the men work at the factory in Townsend, but a waitress over there says otherwise. Who do you think was lying?"

The man said nothing. Nova wasn't surprised. He pretty much figured this was how things were going to go, but he wanted to try to reason with the man before he took more extreme measures.

"Look, I get it. You're a tough guy. I know, because I'm a tough guy. You hear about what happened at the bar last night? Maybe you were even there. I'm the guy who took on three Marines. Yeah, I know they were Marines, just as I know you're a Marine, too."

Nothing. Not even a slight widening of the eyes. The man was a blank slate.

"We could play the whole intimidation game, but I'm guessing that wouldn't lead to much. We could even ratchet it up to torture, but I'm guessing that wouldn't lead to much, either. I mean, maybe after a while you would break, but who's to say what you told me then would even be the truth? Fact is, I'm not even supposed to be here. I'm supposed to be in California by now, but my car—"

Nothing had changed in the man's eyes, but it didn't need to. Pieces of the puzzle were already starting to fall into place. Part of it was realizing that the faint noise he heard was the traffic out on the highway over the ridge. The other part was the XM2010.

Nova looked at the man. He looked at the hut, where inside the sniper rifle rested in its case. He looked up at the ridge.

Nova said, "Tell me I'm reaching."

Finally, a slight change in expression, the man frowning because he didn't know what Nova meant. Of course he didn't. Nova hadn't spoken his theory out loud yet.

"Don't move. I'll be right back."

Nova stood up and started toward the top of the ridge. The moment he looked out at the highway snaking across the desert he knew this was the right place. He recognized the spot, farther down near the asphalt. He couldn't be one hundred percent certain on the location, but it was pretty close to where he had broken down last night. First one tire, then the second, both going flat on the same side of the car. The side facing the ridge on which Nova now stood.

Nova took a final swallow of the Gatorade while he climbed back down to the hut. He tossed the empty bottle aside and again sat down on the rock.

"Okay, so you're running some kind of scam, is that it? You sit up here and take out cars—expensive ones, I'm guessing, cars with only one person inside—and you force them to break down in the middle of nowhere. They try to use their phones to call for help, but there is no service. What—you guys use some kind of cell blocker? Yeah, I guess you would have to. It's the only thing that makes sense. So then with no way to call for help, the driver doesn't know how far the next town up is, so they head back to Parrot Spur on foot. End up at the diner or the bar, get a room at the motel. They might want to call for a tow immediately, but someone feeds them a bullshit story about how the mechanic shop in Townsend is short-staffed and they won't get to it any time soon. Maybe even the sheriff helpfully drives them into town and sets them up with a sweet deal on a used car. All the while the driver calls his insurance and reports the car stolen, because while he's been in Parrot Spur, someone else has come along and picked up the car. In fact ..."

Nova shook his head slowly, then laughed.

"Goddamn. It was that first tractor-trailer that passed me, wasn't it? There are two other tractor-trailers in town, but none of those men are actual truckers. Which begs the question, just what are all of them doing in town? This little scam you have running here stealing cars, it's impressive, but it doesn't take a whole town to pull it off. You probably have people paid off in Townsend, and maybe even people at the insurance companies, because if so many cars start breaking down in one particular spot in Nevada and end up stolen, that will raise a lot of eyebrows. Unless those reports get filed in a special folder or something, am I right?"

The man said nothing, but he didn't need to say anything for Nova to know he was right. He might not have all the details straight, but they were enough to paint a solid enough picture of recent events. Except, the more he thought about it, the scam raised more questions than answers. Especially the amount of ex-military men in town. That number was still bugging him.

In his pocket, his cell phone vibrated.

Nova went to reach for it when he realized that it wasn't his cell phone—his iPhone had since lost battery power—but the man's cell phone. He pulled it out, and despite the fact the phone was locked, a text message could easily be read on the screen.

COME TO MINE ASAP.

"What's at the mine?" Nova asked, looking up just in time to see the rock flying at his face.

It struck him in the temple and knocked him back. He lost his balance and fell off the rock, nearly fell down the incline but caught himself with his foot against the rock he had been sitting on. Pulling himself back up, he saw the man had broken the zip-tie keeping his wrists bound—probably wore it down on a rock until it snapped—and was currently hopping toward the hut. Nova scrambled back to his feet and ran forward just as the man reached the nail gun. He bent and picked it up and aimed it at Nova as Nova charged forward. Just as the man squeezed the trigger, Nova ducked, leaned to the left, then threw himself at the man as he went to fire the nail gun again.

They went right into the steel hut, collapsing the wall, bringing down the roof, the two portable fans tipping over and blowing dirt everywhere.

The man tried to bring up the nail gun but Nova knocked it from his hands and punched him in the face. The man pushed Nova off of him and tried to stand up, but he was at a disadvantage with his ankles bound like they were and fell back down. But he landed near the rifle case, and immediately went to open it. By that point Nova was back on his feet. He saw what the man intended to do. He stepped forward and grabbed the man by the back of his shirt and pulled him to his feet. The man took another swing at Nova. Nova ducked it and planted a right cross to the man's jaw. The man stumbled back, his ankles still bound, trying to keep his balance. He teetered on the edge of the incline for an instant, swinging his arms to stay upright, but gravity had other ideas and he tumbled backward.

Nova took his time making it to the edge of the incline. The last thing he wanted to do was continue this fight. He was tired and he was cranky and he was thirsty again. He didn't want to kill the man, but it was starting to look more and more like he would have no other choice.

But then he looked over the incline and saw he didn't have to do anything. The man had landed headfirst on a boulder thirty feet below. Judging by the awkward angle of the man's head and shoulder, his neck had been snapped. Blood was beginning to pool around his head. His eyes were still open, staring blankly up at the sky.

"Damn," Nova said. "And just when we were becoming friends."

He turned back to the collapsed hut. He opened the rifle case, checked the rifle and the bullets and the rest of the equipment just to be safe. He closed the case and picked it up, along with the canvas bag, and started back toward the trail when he remembered the cooler and grabbed the two bottles of water. Then with everything bundled together, he started down the trail to the dirt bike, barely even glancing at the dead man as he passed him.

23

Jessica heard the helicopter before the two men did. That was probably because they were talking about one thing or another—she had long stopped listening—and the one kept smoking cigarette after cigarette, a collection of butts scattered on the ground by his feet.

She sat in the shade of a pickup truck, her back against the tire, her wrists and ankles bound, duct tape over her mouth, completely scared out of her mind. She had known coming here was a risk, and she had fooled herself into thinking that she could handle the risk if push came to shove, but never once did she imagine she would be in this position. She felt helpless, alone, trapped, certain that her life was soon going to end. Why the men were keeping her alive, she wasn't completely sure, but sooner or later they would be done with her and kill her and probably bury her body somewhere out in the desert.

And then, the helicopter—she heard it before the two men, a distant and near-silent thudding carried on the wind.

A spark of hope flared in her soul. Could this be the police? The DEA? *Someone* to come and rescue her?

But then, just as quickly, she realized that nobody knew she had come here in the first place. She hadn't told anyone, because she didn't want to risk having the wrong questions asked. She knew if her parents found out they would forbid her to do such a stupid, reckless thing. And while Jessica didn't live under their roof anymore and was free to make her own decisions, she most likely would have complied with their wishes. Because in the back of her mind she had always known this was a stupid, reckless thing to do. And still she had done it, and now look at the outcome—tied up on the ground, guarded by two men with guns, while a helicopter was fast approaching.

The smoker immediately dropped his cigarette on the ground. He had barely taken two drags on it. He used the heel of his boot to create a small hole, then kicked the used butts into the hole before covering it back up. The other man just stood there watching him, shaking his head tiredly.

The distant thudding grew and grew until, suddenly, the helicopter appeared over the ridge. It wasn't the police or military or DEA. It was a private helicopter. It circled the bowl twice before leveling out and beginning its descent to a flat section of ground. Dirt flew everywhere. The two men held their hands up in front of their faces to protect their eyes. Jessica, her hands bound behind her back, had to close her eyes, turn her face away, and bury it into her shoulder.

Eventually the roar of the helicopter's engines quieted. The dirt settled. The two men waited where they were, guarding Jessica as if she was some kind of flight risk. She doubted she could very much stand up on her own, let alone try to hop more than ten feet before falling.

Out of the helicopter emerged two men. One wore a tan suit without a tie. Another wore khakis and a polo shirt. The one in the suit had sunglasses on his face and walked just ahead of the man in the polo, who trailed him like an assistant. Clearly the man in the suit was the boss.

The boss reached them and nodded to the two men without a word. He looked down at Jessica, just stared for a moment, before he took off his sunglasses and moved to stand directly in front of her.

Crouching down so he was eye level, he said, "This isn't how you thought today would turn out, is it?"

Jessica, of course, could not answer with the duct tape over her mouth. She just stared back at him, forcing herself not to break eye contact first.

The man looked to be in his late-thirties. His eyes were blue. His head was shaved like the others. Clearly he had been in the military at some point, but Jessica couldn't even begin to guess what branch. She didn't have the same gift John did. And thinking of John, she wondered where he was. Why hadn't she pressed him to come along with her? No doubt if she had, she wouldn't be here right now.

The man reached out, slowly, showing her he wasn't a threat. His fingers pinched one corner of the duct tape. In a smooth, quick motion, he pulled the tape off her mouth.

"There," he said, balling the tape into a small nugget, "that's better. Now I can get a chance to see your gorgeous smile."

Jessica didn't smile.

"Come on," he said, "can't you smile for me?"

She just stared back at him.

"We told you," one of the men said, the smoker, "the bitch won't say a word."

"For starters," the man said, his focus on Jessica, "she's not a bitch. She's not a dyke or cunt or any other derogatory term your small brain manages to think up. She's a young lady who just happened to be in the wrong place at the wrong time." He smiled at her. "Isn't that right?"

Jessica said nothing. She wasn't sure what this guy's game was, but she knew better than to trust him.

The man held her stare for several more seconds before he

nodded. "I see. You don't trust me, do you? No reason you should, not after the way you've been treated. But I'm telling you, nothing bad will happen to you. I just want to know why you were taking pictures of the mine, that's all. Just tell us that and we'll let you go on your way. No harm, no foul. How does that sound?"

The coolness of his voice, the softness of his eyes—Jessica knew it was all an act but she was having trouble not falling for it. The man seemed sincere enough. But he seemed almost *too* sincere, which threw up a red flag. Besides, what was she thinking? Of course this man was bullshitting her. He was the boss, the man in charge, the man who had the ultimate say. He thought he could sweet-talk her into telling him everything she knew, which meant he had done this before. She could just imagine meeting him under different circumstances and falling for his act completely. But not here, not now, bruised and battered with the sticky taste of duct tape still on her lips.

As Jessica's silence continued, the gentleness faded from the man's eyes.

"You don't know anything about me," he said, "but I don't like hurting women. That's not to say I'm above it. In the past I've done things I'm not proud of to get information I need. Sometimes I did those things to women. As you can probably imagine, they weren't pleasant things." He leaned forward, his gaze burning into her. "You're an attractive young woman. I bet you want to maintain that attractiveness, don't you?"

It was uncanny to watch the man's transformation happen right in front of her eyes. One minute he was a sweet, smooth-talking gentleman. The next minute he was a sociopath. It was enough to want to make Jessica tell him why she was here, to tell him everything, but she knew once she started she might not stop. Because even when she ran out of things to tell him, he would think she was hiding something more, and he would still torture her. The thought sent a shiver of fear through her body, but she braced herself, thinking of her brother, how she could go about making him proud.

"Fine," the man said, when it was clear Jessica wasn't going to say a word, "if you want to play it like this, then we'll play it like this. But just remember that I warned you. I gave you a chance to make it easy on yourself, and you refused it."

He waited another beat, as if expecting her to break, and when she didn't, he stood up and turned toward the two men.

The smoker asked, "You want us to go get some tools?"

The boss placed the sunglasses back on his face. "Yes."

The smoker started toward the wooden shed. He had only gone ten paces when the boss spoke again.

"Actually, wait. I have a better idea." He was staring at the wide, open space between the pickup trucks and helicopter. "Bring me the Uzi."

24

The two men undid the binds keeping her wrists and ankles bound. They hefted Jessica to her feet and marched her toward the helicopter. She couldn't go at a normal pace, not with her ankle, but the men didn't seem to be in any hurry. At first she thought they were going to put her in the helicopter, fly her somewhere even more remote, but they stopped maybe one hundred yards away. There was nothing there except flat dirt.

"Lay down," the smoker said.

She just looked at him.

"I'm not going to tell you again."

She looked warily back over her shoulder. The assistant was trailing them, a hammer in one hand, something else in his other hand. Behind him, the boss was standing by the vehicles. He had taken off his suit jacket and was rolling up his shirt-sleeves.

"Please don't do this," Jessica whispered without moving her lips. She shifted her eyes from the smoker to the other man. "Please just let me go."

"Look," the other man said, "now she talks."

The smoker stepped up close to her, leaning forward so he was looking her straight in the eye. "This whole thing is up to you. If you don't want this to happen, then tell Mr. Connolly what he wants to know."

"Rick," the other man said, an explicit warning.

"What?" Rick said. "You think at this point it matters if she knows his name? Shit, now she knows my name, too. And his name?" he said to her, tilting his head toward the other man. "His name is Mike. So now you know everybody's name, but we still don't know yours. You want to rectify that?"

Jessica said nothing.

Rick snorted. "I have to hand it to her," he said to Mike, "she's stronger than she looks."

"We'll see," Mike said. He motioned her to the ground again. "Lay down."

Jessica considered running away. Finally, after several hours, her wrists and ankles were unbound and she was free to do as she wished. But where would she go? Obviously she'd head toward the entrance to the bowl, to the dirt road leading to the highway. But she knew she wouldn't get far. Either the men would chase after her and be even more pissed off for chasing her twice, or they would cut their losses and just shoot her in the back.

But the assistant had reached them and Jessica now saw what it was he carried. Besides the hammer, she recognized the steel metal wickets as the same kind her family used when they set up croquet in the backyard during the summer when she was a girl. Then they had used nine wickets, Jessica and her brother teaming up against their parents. Here now the assistant only had four, and it was suddenly clear what purpose they served.

"Lay down," Mike ordered.

Jessica lowered herself down onto the ground. The sunbaked dirt seared her skin.

She stared up at the sky as the men secured her hands and

feet with the wickets. First Rick used the hammer, then Mike, then they handed it back to the assistant who turned and started away without a word.

"Last chance," Rick said.

Jessica said nothing.

The crunch of dirt off to the side, and a voice said, "That will be all, fellas."

The men turned away and started back toward the vehicles. The boss—Connolly—stepped up beside her.

"I spent much of my military career in the desert. There were days when there was nothing to do. After a while me and the rest of my platoon started throwing around ideas and, well, that's how I came up with bullet rain."

He hefted the Uzi in his hand.

"Do you know anything about guns? No, of course not. This is a mini Uzi. It shoots nine-millimeter Parabellum bullets. Currently the magazine is fully loaded with twenty of these bullets. Its effective range is about one hundred meters. In the desert we were all tough guys, but bullet rain set the boys apart from the men. It showed whether or not we had any fear."

He crouched down, smiling.

"Have you figured it out yet? It's actually quite simple. We would lie down on the ground, aim our guns straight up at the sky, and just let loose. I'm not going to tell you whether or not any of those guys ever ended up shooting themselves, but I will say wind velocity plays a major factor. I might hold this Uzi straight up, and the bullets might shoot straight up, but that doesn't mean they'll fall straight down. And if they do happen to hit you, they might not kill you. Or they might. It's really impossible to say for sure. Now, before we begin, I'll give you one more chance. Tell me why you were out here taking pictures."

Jessica, despite the fact she very much wanted to tell this man everything, said nothing.

"Very well." Connolly stood up. "Before we begin, though, just to make sure you know this isn't a bluff ..."

He aimed the Uzi toward the ground past Jessica and squeezed the trigger. Several bullets tore into the ground, the dirt puffing up with each shot.

"Final chance," Connolly said. "Tell me why you were out here taking pictures. Otherwise I'm going to shoot at the sky and run for cover. It's only going to be a short burst, but a short burst might be all it will take."

Jessica stared up at him. Her entire body trembled. Her lips were even trembling when she opened her mouth to speak.

"Fuck you."

Connolly's smile went tight. He aimed the Uzi straight up in the air. "As you wish."

Jessica closed her eyes. She didn't want to see what happened next.

A single gunshot rang out in the silence.

Jessica opened her eyes and watched the Uzi fall to the ground.

Connolly stood there, stunned, staring at his bleeding hand. "What the fuck?"

That was when the helicopter exploded.

25

Nova peered through the scope and watched the three others by the vehicles. Two of them grabbed for weapons, while the other one—the guy in the polo shirt, what looked to be an assistant—jerked his head around frantically searching for cover. Nova knew the assistant wasn't a threat, so he touched the trigger and placed a bullet in one of the other men's legs. The man cried out and went down. Nova shifted the rifle toward the other armed man, but by then the man had dove behind a pickup truck.

Nova scrambled to his feet, shouldering the XM2010, and sprinted toward where he had stashed the dirt bike. The canvas bag hung off the handlebar. He slipped it over his shoulder as he kick-started the bike, revved the engine, then released the clutch. The rear tire kicked up dirt as he went up and over the ridge. There was a second or two where he caught air and thought it a very good chance he might lose control. But he had picked this location for a reason—the smooth slope—and as gravity brought the bike back down, Nova leaned forward and rode straight down to the base of the bowl.

The explosion had forced the man in the suit to the ground. The dropped Uzi lay a couple feet away. Nova veered straight for it, pushing the dirt bike for all it was worth, and he was only yards away when movement caught his attention by the mine entrance. Two more men had appeared and were firing at him. Nova slowed just long enough to drop the XM2010 from his shoulder. He took aim and shot both men—one in the shoulder, the other in the leg—before tossing the spent rifle aside.

He gunned the engine again and zoomed forward. The fiery ball that was the helicopter began billowing black smoke. He could feel the heat even from over one hundred yards away. Jessica was still on the ground, trapped, screaming for help. Nova slid to a stop beside her, leaned down and snatched the Uzi from the ground. He brought it back up just as one of the men started shooting at him.

Nova returned fire, letting off only a few bursts. He didn't have any spare magazines and didn't want to waste the ammunition. He moved the bike so it was between Jessica and the men. He propped the bike on the kickstand and bent to yank the two metal wires keeping Jessica's wrists to the ground. She sat up, dislodged the wires keeping her ankles in place, and scrambled to her feet.

"Who the fuck are you?"

The man in the suit was climbing to his feet. He held his right hand close to his chest, the shirt soaked with blood.

Nova aimed the Uzi at the man's face. "I'm just a guy," he said. Then to Jessica: "Get on."

There wasn't much room but she climbed onto the back of the dirt bike, wrapping her arms around him and holding him tight.

The man in the suit said, "You're dead."

Nova winked at him. "Do me a favor and step to the side."

"What?"

He gunned the engine again. The front wheel lifted as they

bolted forward, headed for the only exit to the bowl, Nova letting off another three-round burst from the Uzi at the men by the vehicles to give them time.

The dirt road leading from the mine to the highway wasn't a straight shot. Still Nova put the dirt bike in high gear, certain that at least one of the men would be coming after them. It was only as they got halfway down the road, the highway in sight ahead of them, did a pickup truck turn in off the highway.

Nova let off on the gas, slowing the bike to a halt. The pickup coming at them was maybe five hundred yards away.

Jessica screamed, "Look out!"

He glanced over his shoulder and saw two men on dirt bikes cresting the ridge from the bowl.

"Hold on," Nova shouted.

Jessica leaned in even closer, her arms tight around his chest.

He gunned the engine again, the rear tire kicking up more dirt, and steered them off the road into the desert.

26

Jessica held on as tightly as she could, the dirt bike bouncing up and down as they sped across the rough terrain. She worried that if she lost her grip for only an instant, she would tumble off the back of the bike. She glanced back over her shoulder and saw the two men on the dirt bikes not too far away, the pickup right behind them.

"Hold on!" John shouted at her again, and leaned the bike toward the right, in the direction of the highway.

The desert here was open, only slight vegetation, and they zoomed toward the thin strip of macadam in the distance.

They didn't get far before the ground beside them began spitting up dirt.

Jessica screamed.

John slowed at once, the dirt bike wobbling back and forth like it might tip over. Then, before she knew it, the bike was doing a complete one-eighty, and the men on the dirt bikes behind them were suddenly in front of them.

As they zoomed forward, John raised the Uzi and fired off several more three-round bursts.

Neither man was hit, but they both ducked, and one of them lost control of his bike and went flying over the handlebars.

John kept driving forward, back toward the mine, aiming now at the pickup which was moving in a wide circle to catch up with them. He paused only briefly, the engine still growling, and carefully aimed the Uzi before squeezing off a few more shots at the pickup.

Jessica watched the windshield become pocked with bullets before shattering completely.

The pickup slid to a halt, dust flying everywhere. The passenger door was flung open and one of the men jumped out, rolling to the ground and firing back at them.

John didn't waste any time. He got them moving again, the dirt bike's engine whining loudly. Now they weren't headed back toward the mine so much as the mountains past the mine.

Jessica, still holding on tightly, once again looked back over her shoulder.

The man who had tumbled off his bike was back on, and both men were speeding after them. They were trying to keep up, and John led them through the desert, the bike bouncing again, Jessica certain she would lose her grip at any moment.

Pretty soon they headed down into a ditch, and John skidded to a halt. He pushed down the kickstand and stepped away from the bike.

He asked, "You okay?"

Jessica forced herself to nod.

John dropped the Uzi's magazine to check how many rounds were left. Then he clicked it back in place, holding a finger of his free hand up to his lips for her to be quiet. The sound of the approaching dirt bikes was growing closer and closer. John turned away from her, aiming the Uzi at the top of the ridge.

It wasn't long before the first dirt bike, then the second, appeared over the ridge and headed down into the ditch.

John squeezed off the rest of the rounds, and both men fell right off their bikes.

He tossed the Uzi aside and headed toward the closest man on the ground. A gun lay only yards away from where it had been dropped. John picked it up and held it on the man while he looked over at where the other man had fallen. That man didn't move, his face down in the dirt. Even from Jessica's vantage point, it was clear the man had been shot dead.

But the man John was standing over was still alive. He had been shot in his side, blood soaking his shirt. He tried to turn over, his one hand on the wound, his other hand pushing off the ground.

John asked, "What's your name?"

"Fuck you," the man spat, blood dribbling down his chin.

"You know, your sniper friend said the same thing to me. Actually, he didn't say much, but I could see it in his eyes. He's dead now, in case you were wondering."

The man turned over onto his back, groaning in the pain. "You can kill me, I don't care. Either way, you're a dead man. You and the bitch. You think you're going to walk away from this alive? They're going to hunt you down. They're going to tear you apart. They're going to—"

The single gunshot was sudden and loud, startling her.

The man groaned again, his other hand moving to the new wound in his knee.

John lowered the gun and said, "You talk too much."

"Fuck you," the man spat again.

A moment of silence passed, and in that moment Jessica heard the oncoming pickup truck. Judging by the sound, it wasn't that far away.

"John!" she called, and when he looked at her, she gestured up at the top of the ridge.

"I hear them. Stay there," he said, and started up the incline.

Jessica watched him go, speechless, wondering what the hell

he thought he was doing, then wondering what she would do if he didn't come back. She didn't know how to ride a dirt bike. And the man on the ground was still alive. What if he managed to get to his feet? What if he came after her?

She watched the top of the ridge. Listening to the man groan in pain. Listening to the approaching pickup truck. She heard the crack of gunfire. Then more gunfire. Then even more gunfire.

Someone cried out.

Someone else shouted.

More gunfire.

Then silence.

She waited, listening past the man groaning in pain, past the wind, past the echoing in her ears.

Nothing.

Except ... there was something. Footsteps. Footsteps headed this way.

Jessica swallowed. She wasn't sure what to do. The dead man had a weapon on him, didn't he? Yes, there had to be one on him, and if not on him, then somewhere nearby. She could run over there—or hobble, if that's what it took. She could find his weapon. She could—

John appeared then, standing at the top of the ridge, before starting to make his way down. He had a rifle slung over his shoulder, two pistols in each hand.

"Two more pickups are headed this way," he said. "We won't be able to head back to the highway, so we need to keep going into the hills." He nodded toward the one dirt bike. "You know how to drive?"

She shook her head.

"Okay," John said. He turned back to the man. "Do me a favor?"

"Fuck you."

John ignored this. "Tell your boss the guy that blew up his

helicopter has a message for him. Tell him I hope he has good insurance."

The man said, "He's going to kill you."

John secured the pistols in the back of his jeans and threw a leg over the dirt bike. He kick-started the engine again, flicked the kickstand up, and without even a glance back at the man, drove them away.

27

Connolly checked the bandage on his hand. It was starting to bleed through again.

"Towel," he said, snapping his fingers at the men crowded around him.

A fresh towel was promptly placed in his hand. He unwrapped the towel around his other hand—the wounded hand, his gun hand, for Christ's sake—and let it fall to the ground. He was going to need stitches, no doubt about it. It was going to leave a scar, too. He didn't much care about an extra scar—he had more than his fair share—but what worried him most was that he might not be able to shoot as well with the hand as he had previously.

Wrapping the fresh towel around the wound, he turned to the men spread out around him. Only a half dozen at the moment, but more would be coming soon. A few had already started off into the desert in the pickup trucks. Samuel had tried calling those men, but none had answered yet. Connolly knew that might mean they were in heavy pursuit, but a nagging feeling told him otherwise.

"How much longer would you like to wait?" Samuel asked.

Connolly watched the other men, already decked out in gear. They were loading weapons, extra magazines, even sheathing knives.

"A few more minutes at the most," Connolly said. "How long before the rest get here?"

"Should be soon."

Connolly cleared his throat. The men quieted and turned to him.

"I need two volunteers to continue with the delivery. In fact, all the product that we have needs to be loaded up and taken to the drop-off site ASAP."

None of the men said anything. Connolly couldn't blame them. Their existences had become routine, and something like this—a hunt—was too much to pass up.

He waited another moment, then pointed at two men and said, "Sorry, fellas, you just pulled the short straws."

The men didn't look happy about it, but they didn't complain. Their complaints would come later, in the SUVs, and as far as Connolly was concerned, that was fine by him. He had been a soldier, once upon a time. He knew what kind of things soldiers said about their commanding officers. Even though this wasn't the military, it followed the same basic principles, and even though Connolly was no general, he was still the top dog.

As he went to say something else to the men, the phone in Samuel's hand chirped.

Samuel placed the phone to his ear, spoke briefly, listened for several long seconds, then disconnected the call. When he turned toward Connolly, the news was apparent on his face.

"How many?" Connolly asked.

"Three dead. Rick is still alive."

"Wounded?"

A slight nod. "Shot a few times."

"Did he say anything?"

Samuel's eyes shifted away.

"Well?"

Samuel cleared his throat. "He said the guy who blew up your helicopter says he hopes you have good insurance."

The helicopter was still on fire, billowing smoke. It would die down eventually. It wasn't like there were any fire trucks nearby. And if there were, it wasn't like many could make it up the dirt road to the mine. Even if they could, where were they going to get water? Besides, Connolly rather liked the fact the helicopter was still on fire. Every time the wind shifted and the smoke drifted this way, he thought more and more how he was going to love killing this asshole.

"They have any idea where he and the girl are headed now?"

"Rick said they were headed north, toward the canyons."

"Well," Connolly said, both to himself and to the men around him, "lucky for us that's the middle of nowhere. They'll be headed either for Townsend or Kadrey. My money's on Kadrey, because it's closer, but even then there isn't much in town that will help them. Our local law enforcement friends have already been alerted and are keeping an ear to the ground. Trust me, fellas, these two aren't going to get far. As of right now, they've been lucky. But their luck is soon going to run out."

Nods of agreement all around, but the men were silent. Waiting like good soldiers.

"It's going to get dark within the next three hours. We have equipment that will help us in the dark. These two don't. Fact is, they don't have jack shit. We're going to find them, but we're not going to kill them. Not yet. Got it?"

Another round of nods.

The phone in Samuel's hand chirped again.

Samuel placed the phone to his ear, listened for a moment, then disconnected the call. He turned toward Connolly, opened his mouth, but hesitated. That was the one thing Connolly couldn't stand about the man, the constant hesitation.

This wasn't his world. Samuel had never been in the Army. He had gone to an Ivy League school, had been working on Wall Street when Connolly came across him and offered him a job. The man was good at what he did, knowing how to launder money, but besides that, he was expendable.

"Who was that?" Connolly asked.

"Pete."

They had sent Pete out earlier to check on Joe, who had been out in the desert already for some reason. The way it was explained to Connolly, Joe had a dirt bike and sniper rifle, both of which the asshole had shown up with, so it was assumed something had happened to the man. Only it still hadn't been explained to Connolly what Joe was doing with the dirt bike and sniper rifle, or why he was out in the desert in the first place.

"And?"

Samuel shook his head.

This time the men offered up angry murmurs.

One of the men asked, "Did they find his phone?"

Samuel shook his head again.

Connolly thought about that for a moment. He still wasn't sure what it was Joe had been up to—and once this mess was taken care of, that was the first thing he was going to demand answers for—but if the asshole had shown up with Joe's dirt bike and sniper rifle, then it was a safe bet the asshole had Joe's phone now, too.

"Call it," Connolly said.

28

Nova squeezed the brake until the dirt bike came to a complete stop. He didn't have much choice. They had run out of room— at least room for the dirt bike to squeeze through.

It had only been a few minutes since they entered the canyons. Maneuvering through the tight corridors had been tricky, but he had managed. Now there was nowhere to go but back. Problem was, back was where the people hunting them were.

There was a sliver in the rock ahead of them, just enough room for one person to squeeze through at a time. It looked to go back several yards before it widened again.

The canyon walls stretched up toward the sky around them, at least one hundred yards tall.

Nova let the engine idle for a couple of seconds, then killed it.

Jessica asked, "Why are we stopping?"

He tilted his head to look back at her, placed a finger to his lips.

Silence.

It wasn't a normal silence, not the kind most people were accustomed to where there was always some kind of background noise, whether it be distant traffic or air blowing through a vent or the faint, high-pitched whine of electronics. This silence was a deep, all-encompassing silence that had existed since the beginning of time.

The silence was so strong that Nova even found himself holding his breath. He heard blood singing in his ears and Jessica's shallow breathing, and beyond that, the sound of engines. More dirt bikes, without a doubt, but probably more pickup trucks, too ... though he doubted any of them would venture far down here.

"Do you hear that?"

Jessica, her face frozen, her eyes narrowed, nodded slightly.

"If we can hear them, they can hear us."

"Where'd the dirt bikes come from anyway?"

"I figure from that wooden shed outside the mine entrance." He glanced down at her ankle. "What happened there?"

"I fell when those men were chasing me."

"Sprained?"

"I think so."

"How much walking do you think you can do on it?"

She bit her lip, paused a beat. "Maybe a little. But I don't think I could go too far. I can put some pressure on it, but not a lot. You want us to go through there, don't you?"

She didn't bother indicating the sliver in the canyon wall.

Nova started to nod, started to say something, when the phone in his pocket began to vibrate.

He paused, wondering how that was even possible. His phone was dead. Then, like before, he realized it wasn't his phone—it was the sniper's. He pulled it from his pocket and glanced at the screen.

"Who's that?" Jessica asked.

"No idea."

There was no name on the screen, just the words INCOM-ING CALL. Nova was surprised the phone even got service this far out and noted the one bar.

"Are you going to answer it?"

The phone vibrated again in his hand. In the distance, the sound of the dirt bikes was getting closer. They were maybe another half mile away. The canyons were a maze, but if Nova and Jessica stayed stationary, the men would find them soon.

Nova pressed the green button and placed the phone to his ear.

"If this is a telemarketer, I'm not interested."

A beat of silence on the other end, and then a voice said, "Is this the asshole who blew up my helicopter?"

"That depends. Which helicopter was yours?"

"You're in over your head."

"So let me get this straight—you're not a telemarketer?"

Another beat of silence. "I guess this is the part where I'm supposed to threaten you, isn't it?"

"If this is who I think it is, you already threatened me. Told me I'm dead, if I'm not mistaken."

"That was a moment of weakness on my part. Men who threaten are usually those without control."

"Did you read that in a fortune cookie?"

"I'm a businessman, to tell you the truth, and when I see potential, I know better than to disrespect it."

"I don't think I get your drift," Nova said. The dirt bikes, he realized, were getting even closer. "You want to offer me a job?"

"There are quite a few recent openings in my organization, no thanks to you. If you wanted to fill one of those openings, I would be more than happy to consider it."

Nova laughed. "This is why you called me?"

"I'm taking a chance. Believe it or not, I can be a very reasonable man."

"Right. Says the guy who was about to play bullet rain with an innocent girl tied to the ground."

Another beat of silence. When the voice spoke again, Nova could hear a smile.

"I had a feeling you were once in the service. What branch?"

"Navy. You?"

"Army."

Nova said, "Then I guess we don't like each other on principle."

"How do you know about bullet rain?"

"I'd heard stories. Some Rangers told me about it once in a bar on the outskirts of Kabul."

"Have you ever played?"

Nova laughed again. "Bullet rain is a sucker's game created by some hotheads who wanted to get their kicks off."

The smile dropped from the voice. "Actually, I created bullet rain."

"Bullshit."

"It's true."

"Whatever, man. More power to you."

"I just want the girl."

"I want my car."

Another beat of silence.

"What are you talking about?"

"I'm talking about my goddamn car. Your men stole it, and I want it back."

The silence that ensued was a beat longer than before.

The man said, "I'm not exactly sure what you're talking about, but we can work this out. If my men have in fact stolen your car, I can return it to you. We can do an even trade, your car for the girl."

Nova had to suppress laughter. "Do you honestly think I would ever consider doing that?"

"John, this isn't going to end well for you."

"Who says my name is John?"

"From what I understand, that's what the girl called you before you shot one of my men in the knee."

"She may have called me that, but that's not my name."

"Well whatever your name is, this isn't going to end well for you—you or the girl."

"So wait—you're taking the job off the table?"

"My men are going to find you. They know this terrain. You don't. You're outnumbered. You're outgunned. You might as well make it easy on yourself and surrender."

"When you say it like that, how could I possibly resist?"

"I told you I'm a businessman, didn't I? Nobody fucks with my business."

"Yeah, well, I'm pretty sure I just did."

"And I will kill you for it."

"You should be thanking me, actually."

"For what?"

"Sparing your life. I could have put that bullet in your head, but instead I shot your hand."

"I was wondering about that. Why didn't you kill me?"

"I'm trying to be a better person."

The dirt bikes were even closer now. Jessica kept looking back over her shoulder, her face growing anxious by the second.

"Look," Nova said into the phone, "I would love to continue our chat, but right now I'm in the middle of something. Give me your number and I'll fax over my resume and maybe we can talk later about setting up an official interview."

The man went to say something else, but Nova disconnected the call. He tore the battery from the phone, tossed both pieces away, said to Jessica, "Think you can squeeze through there?"

Again, no need to indicate the sliver in the canyon wall.

Jessica nodded apprehensively.

"Then get going," Nova said. "They'll be here any minute."

29

There were only three men on dirt bikes. None of them wore helmets. Each of them had a rifle slung over his shoulder. They weren't going fast, not as fast as Nova had been going, but that was because the lead rider was concentrating on the dirt, following Nova's tracks. The growl of their engines reverberated off the canyon walls and made the loose dirt nearby shiver in anticipation.

The sky was clear and fading, the sun nearing the horizon. Shadows stretched across the desert, especially down here in the canyons.

The men on the dirt bikes turned the corner and the first one slowed and raised a fist, alerting the two men behind him.

The other two stopped, lowered their kickstands, and slipped the rifles off their shoulders.

Farther ahead they saw the solitary dirt bike, the one they had been chasing.

Beyond the dirt bike they saw the sliver in the canyon wall and the shape of a young woman trying to squeeze herself through.

The first man killed his engine, and the two others killed their engines, too.

The first man shouted, "Hey!"

Jessica looked back through the sliver at the men. Her eyes were wide with fear. She no doubt had heard the men coming—had even known they were right there—but the sound of the man's voice was enough to spook her.

A few more feet and she would make it to the other side. She was playing up her sprained ankle, limping more than she probably needed to. Clearly there was more than enough room for her to squeeze through, but the men didn't seem to notice. They had been sent to track her down, and here they had found her, and she was so very close.

The first man lowered the kickstand to his dirt bike, climbed off as he unslung the rifle and held it with both hands. As he began to advance, he said, "Where is he?"

The other two men, their rifles now held at the ready and advancing behind the first man, began looking around the canyon walls, and Jessica, no doubt noticing this, decided to improvise.

She screamed.

It was enough to stop all three men. The barrels of their rifles momentarily dipped toward the ground. All of their attention was now focused on the girl as she shuffled the last couple of feet to the other side.

The first man repeated his question. "Where is he?"

Jessica screamed again.

The men, having momentarily been taken aback, began to raise their weapons.

At that same moment, Nova dropped down to the ground behind them. The canyon walls narrowed the higher they went. That was where Nova had climbed up only minutes ago. Then, his hands and feet pressed against the sides, he had lowered himself more and more as the men advanced closer to the sliver and to Jessica. Now he dropped maybe fifteen feet, rolling as he hit the ground to take the stress off his legs, pulling the pistol from the waistband of his jeans and aiming it at the men.

Before, he had been on the fence whether or not to take any lives, but now it was crystal clear: these men were going to kill him unless he killed them first.

He fired off six rounds, two bullets per man. One head shot, one chest shot. None of the men had time to even squeeze their own triggers. They each dropped to the ground.

Nova stood up straight, feeling the tension in his legs. He should have climbed down a couple more feet before making the drop. He had been lucky. The last thing he needed was to sprain his ankle just like Jessica. They'd be sitting ducks then for sure.

He lowered the pistol to his side and started forward, toward the three dead men. He noted their rifles and their sidearms. He also noted the walkie-talkies each had clipped to their belts.

He bent toward the first man, reaching for his walkie-talkie, when Jessica shouted, "John, watch out!"

He fell to the ground at once, rolling to the side, raising the pistol again and squeezing off one round at the man behind him.

His shot echoed off the canyon walls a half-second after the man's shot did.

The man had been using a rifle, and his shot had been close to Nova—shards of the canyon wall beside him burst everywhere—but Nova's bullet had gone straight through the man's throat.

The man stared ahead, choking on his own blood, before falling to his knees, then down onto his face.

Nova hurried toward the new dead man and the three dirt bikes. He peeked around the canyon wall, saw another dirt bike propped up with its kickstand. The fourth man must have been farther away and pushed it forward on the off chance something like this would happen.

When he was sure the coast was clear—that deep silence again enveloping the area—Nova returned to the three dead men. By that point Jessica was making her way back through the sliver.

Nova took one of the walkie-talkies off a belt, turned the volume down to almost silent, then clipped it to his own belt.

Jessica limped toward him, the canvas bag now strapped over her chest. Judging by her pace and the distance and the time it took before she reached him, Nova wouldn't have been surprised if a desert tortoise sped past her.

"Are you okay?" she asked.

He nodded. "You?"

She grimaced at the pain. "I've been better."

Then as she neared her eyes took in all the death and Nova saw something change in her face, a mixture of revulsion and relief.

"My God," she whispered. "They're just … *gone*, aren't they? One second they were alive, and now they're gone."

Nova stood back up, shouldering another rifle, and offered the other to Jessica. She just stared at it for the longest time before numbly taking it from him.

"It was either them or us," he said, "and quite frankly, I'm glad it was them."

She swallowed, her eyes focused on the dead bodies, and nodded. "Now what?"

"Others are coming. Maybe not right away, but they'll be here soon."

"So should we do the same thing again, with me back there and you up there?"

Nova shook his head. "We were lucky this time, that's all. It might not go down the same way again. Besides, we can't just wait here forever. The sun will be down within the hour. It's going to get dark and cold real soon."

"So what do you think we should do?"

"I remember passing a town a couple miles before Parrot Spur."

"That would be Kadrey."

"Right. I think we should head that way."

She glanced back at the cell phone he had tossed earlier. "Why don't we just call the police?"

"There's a chance the local law is corrupt. In fact, I know the local law is corrupt. The same could be true of a few state troopers. We can't take the risk."

"So then what are we supposed to do?"

"If we can make it to Kadrey and get to a phone, there's someone I know who might be able to help."

She gestured to the cell phone and battery on the ground. "Why not use that?"

"It was locked. And mine is dead. And if any of these men are carrying cell phones, they'll be locked, too. Besides, there's a very good chance they'll be tracking the phones very soon, if they aren't already."

She looked around the area again, taking in the dead bodies and the blood soaking the dirt. "We can't just ride one of the dirt bikes again, can we?"

"Not unless we want them to find us."

"So then what are we going to do? I can't walk very fast. It'll take forever for us to get to Kadrey."

"I know," Nova said. "That's why I'm going to carry you."

30

Connolly disconnected the call, held the cell phone in his hand for a moment, then turned and flung it at the wall.

Behind him, Sheriff Leonard Smith said, "What happened?"

Connolly spun around, his face red, glaring down at the sheriff. Then the fire went out of his eyes, and he sighed. "Four more of my men are dead."

"Jesus Christ."

"They found them in the canyons. Three of them had bullets in their heads, one in the throat."

"Their bikes?"

"Still there, plus the one the asshole and the girl were using."

"Which means they're now on foot."

Connolly nodded.

"And didn't you say something's wrong with her ankle?"

"Rick said she twisted it when she tried running away the first time. They won't get far."

"What about weapons?"

"Two of the rifles are missing, as are two of the pistols. Some extra ammunition. And a radio. Who is this guy?"

"I have no idea."

"You let him stay in this office last night. You gave him a goddamn ride into Townsend earlier today. You don't know his name?"

"He said his name was John."

"You didn't check his ID?"

"I did and I ran it. Everything seemed legit. If John really isn't his name, then his fake identity is flawless. Besides, I was trying not to make a big deal out of things. The less hassle we gave him, the more I figured he would be ready to just walk away."

Connolly approached the desk, slowly, the fire in his eyes returning. He placed his hands on the edge of the desk and leaned forward. "What the fuck has been going on in this town?"

The sheriff looked away, staring off at a far wall. He took a deep breath. "You've said it time and again, there's always more money to be made."

"What did you do?"

"We saw an opportunity. One of the men we deliver to outside L.A. asked us if we wanted to make more money. He knew our location and said he had friends in the area, friends who could help us. He drew up an entire plan, the number of people needed, just how much each of us would make. The money was just too good to say no."

"You already make more than enough money. Everyone here does."

Now keeping his gaze level with Connolly's, the sheriff said, "There's always more money to be made."

Connolly's nails dug into the desktop, his face burning red. "You are a goddamn hick sheriff in a goddamn hick town. What could you possibly need more money for?"

Before Smith could answer, the door opened and in walked Samuel carrying a notepad. He saw Connolly leaning on the desk, then the pieces of the shattered cell phone on the floor, and paused. "What happened?"

"Four more of our men are dead is what happened," Connolly said, pushing away from the desk. "Did you know about this side operation?"

Samuel hesitated only a beat, but it was more than enough for Connolly.

"I should kill both of you right now," he said. "How long has this been going on?"

A long moment of silence, neither man wanting to answer. Finally Smith said, "Nearly two years."

Connolly turned away, shaking his head, staring up at the ceiling. "Stealing cars. What the fuck were you thinking?"

"They weren't just any cars. They were specific cars. High-value cars. This guy has contacts at every insurance company. He makes sure the insurance companies take the hit and nothing ever comes back on us. Trust me, we're careful. We only choose cars with one driver. We have jammers set up on the highway to block cell reception. There were always questions, and sometimes there were suspicions, but nothing ever came of it. The guy made sure everything ran smoothly."

Connolly turned back around. "You're in contact with this guy?"

Smith nodded hesitantly.

"Find out where the Mustang is. Have them search every inch of it. I want to know who this asshole really is." He paused, took a breath. "Any word on the helicopter?"

Samuel nodded. "It should be here within an hour."

"Good. Have them land it at the mine." He noticed Samuel's notepad. "What have you got there?"

Samuel cleared his throat, looking down at the notepad. "There doesn't seem to be any connection between the man and the girl. She arrived early yesterday afternoon. Said something about driving west and asked if she could get a room. She paid cash."

"ID?"

"No. Not even any credit cards or registration in the glove box. But I called one of our contacts at the DMV and had him run the license plate. Her name is Jessica Hirsch. Her address is Flat Rock, Michigan. She's twenty-two years old."

"That's great, but it doesn't explain why she was taking pictures of the mine."

"Actually," Smith said, his chair squeaking as he leaned forward, "I think it does."

31

The sun had just touched the horizon when John said, "I think we should stop and rest for a bit."

He had been carrying Jessica piggyback most of the time. She had tried walking on her own for a little, but the pressure on her ankle became too much, especially with the terrain as they went up and down and over rocks. The canyons were a maze and they were rats, searching for that elusive piece of cheese, only in this case the rats were also being hunted by several men bent on killing them.

John set her down gently. She lowered herself onto a rock, took the canvas bag strapped across her chest, and placed it on the ground.

"Can I have one of these?" she asked him, pulling out one of the bottles of water.

He nodded without a word as he surveyed their surroundings. They had exited the canyons and were now on level ground. The few rocks and boulders here hid them from their antagonists, but at the same time it hid their antagonists from them. For all they knew, the men hunting them were right over the ridge.

John said, "Wait here. And take this gun."

He was gone for maybe a minute. Jessica sat on the rock, sipping the warm water with one hand while holding the gun with the other hand. Finally John returned.

"I can't see the highway from here, but I think I can see Kadrey off in the distance."

"How much farther?"

"Looks to be a couple more miles. Maybe two, no more than three."

She extended the gun back to him, meaning for him to take it, but he waved it off.

"Keep it," he said. He grabbed the canvas bag off the ground, pulled out his leather jacket, and handed it to her. "Here, put this on."

She set the gun on the rock beside her, took the jacket but didn't put it on. "Why are you doing this?"

"You look cold."

"No, I mean all of this—everything. Why? You don't even know me."

"Sure I do. Your name is Jessica. You drive a ridiculously small car."

She shook her head and looked away, watched as the last remaining arc of the sun dipped below the horizon.

"Look," John said, his voice quiet, "I know this is scary, but everything will be okay. Once we get to Kadrey, I make a call and the cavalry arrives. It's as simple as that."

Now she felt tears in her eyes. "Are you kidding? These guys are going to kill us."

"They haven't killed us yet."

"Who *are* you?"

"I'm just a guy."

"You told Connelly your name isn't really John."

"It isn't. My friends call me Nova. Is Connelly the name of the guy in charge?"

She wiped at her eyes, watched as he started checking the area again, the gun held at his side. "That's what the others called him. The one guy even called him Mr. Connelly, all formal like. When you were on the phone with him, you said you were in the Navy."

"That's right. I was a SEAL."

"What are you now?"

"I told you, I'm between jobs."

"But what did you do before this?"

He hesitated. "I killed people for our country."

"You mean like a spy?"

"This was completely off the books. Totally non-sanctioned. When our government needed full deniability, they called my team in."

"What happened to your team?"

He didn't answer, his back to her, staring out at the horizon.

"You don't have to tell me," she said.

"No, it's just my team ... the whole thing unraveled a while back."

"What do you mean?"

"Two of them went rogue. Another died just the other week outside of Vegas."

"Oh my God. I'm so sorry. That's why you didn't want to drive through Vegas, isn't it? You said because of bad memories."

"He was a really good guy, funny and sweet. Smart, too, a complete genius."

"How did he die?"

"By saving another team member's life."

"So he was a hero."

A thoughtful nod. "That he was."

"What about the rest of your team?"

"There was only one other. She ... well, she got us in trouble sometimes." He smiled. "She believed in a certain form of justice that I normally didn't."

"What do you mean?"

"I'd always been a pretty straightforward guy. There was a job to do, I went in and did it. I didn't worry about the consequences or how it affected others. But Holly"—he shook his head slowly, staring off at the horizon—"she sometimes took things too seriously. She cared too much."

"And that's a bad thing?"

He looked at her again. "In that line of work, yes. The only way to survive is making sure you look out for yourself at all times. It's only when you start caring about others that you might do something stupid and get yourself killed."

Jessica felt the corner of her mouth curling up. "Is that what you're doing now, something stupid?"

"You could say that. The old me would have known there was something screwy about Parrot Spur but wouldn't have cared. After you dropped me off, I started walking around town and the sheriff came and drove me out. He took me to Townsend and more or less tried to sell me on buying a used car and going on my way."

"Why didn't you?"

"Because I had a nagging feeling something wasn't right. I had whatever it is my friend has that gets her into trouble. I knew I should have just bought a car and continued on to California, but instead I came back."

She listened to the cicadas and the wind and the ghostly echoes of all that gunfire. "How did you find me, anyway?"

"I followed dirt bike tracks out of town and it brought me to a man with a sniper rifle. Where he was set up, he had a good view of where my car broke down yesterday."

"You think he had something to do with your tires going flat?"

"I know for a fact he had something to do with my tires

going flat. But this whole thing is more than just stealing cars. The operation is way too big for that. What were you doing at the mine?"

She opened her mouth but didn't speak.

Nova had kept moving around the area this entire time, the gun in his hand, checking to make sure they were safe. Now he turned toward her, and there was something different about his expression, something Jessica didn't like.

"The truth this time," he said. "Not that graduate-student-studying-abandoned-mines bullshit."

Jessica wasn't sure what to say, so she said nothing.

Nova started checking the area again. "I've never been one to believe in coincidences. You ended up at the mine for a reason, just as you almost ended up playing bullet rain."

"That guy you found, the sniper—you killed him?"

"You're avoiding the question."

"Did you kill him?"

"Not on purpose."

"How did you know I was at the mine?"

"I didn't. The sniper got a text telling him to come to the mine ASAP. I took the dirt bike there."

She frowned. "I don't remember hearing a dirt bike until after the helicopter exploded."

"I didn't want the sound of the engine to alert anyone I was coming. I didn't know what I was going to find, if anything. So I cut the engine and pushed it in neutral when I was a half mile away. Managed to hide it behind some bushes nearby. Now why were you there?"

No more stalling.

She closed her eyes, took a deep breath, and said, "I was there because of my brother."

"What about your brother?"

"I think"—her voice cracked, tears in her eyes—"I think they killed him."

32

"His name was Jacob. He was a Ranger. He left the service a year ago and tried finding work, but there just weren't any jobs. Then someone he knew, another Ranger, hooked him up with something. Jacob wouldn't say what the job was, only that the money was good. He was even helping to pay my tuition. But besides that, I never saw or heard from him."

The rock was becoming uncomfortable. She lowered herself onto the ground, the rock now at her back, unscrewing the cap from the bottle and taking a swig of water.

"Occasionally I would get emails from him. They were cryptic. He never said where he was or what he was doing, just that he was living the Dream. When he typed it he even capitalized the word. It was weird. My brother had never been a strong student. That's why he went into the Army instead of college. He used to be a troublemaker, too, and my parents didn't think he was going to last. But still he was my brother. I loved him."

She wiped at her eyes, smiling.

"Like, this one time when I was thirteen, I was at camp and hated it. I called home and Jacob answered and I told him just how much I hated it and how I wanted to leave. And you know what he did? He drove three hours to come pick me up. But I didn't end up going back home with him. He told me I was going to love it at camp if I just stuck it out. And you know what? He was right. I did end up loving it. Later I found out he was supposed to go out on a date that night with a girl he really liked, but instead called it off to drive three hours to talk to me."

There was a silence then, the cicadas trilling around them.

Nova—so weird to think of him now with that name, after thinking of him as John—kept moving around, the gun in his hand, back and forth checking the area. He asked, "What happened to him?"

"One night I got a missed call from him. I had been at class and left my phone in the car. He left a voicemail, though. He said he had really messed up and he was scared."

"Scared of what?"

"He didn't say. He was crying. I had never heard my brother cry before. I had never even heard him say he was scared before. It broke my heart. I wanted to do something, but what was I supposed to do?"

"Did you call him back?"

"I tried. I tried for a whole day. I was freaking out. I thought about telling my parents, but I knew that wouldn't be a good idea. Then the next day I got another call from Jacob. He wasn't crying this time, but he was really on edge. He said they were coming for him. He said they were almost there, and that he was sorry and that he loved me and just wanted to hear my voice one last time."

Jessica sniffed back more tears, took another swig of water.

"I asked him what happened and he said he had fucked up. That's all he kept saying, that he had fucked up. Finally I shouted at him to tell me what was wrong, what he had done. He said he should have known better, he knew it was illegal but it was a job and all he needed was a job."

"What job?"

"Transporting drugs. Meth. He said the people he worked with—all guys from the service—produced it in an abandoned mine. Then he started crying again, saying how sorry he was but that he loved me and missed me and wished he could see me again. And then … then he hung up."

"Did you try calling him back?"

"Of course. That's all I did for hours. But there was no answer. I thought about telling my parents. I thought they might know what to do, but I was just kidding myself. If what Jacob said was true, then this was bigger than my parents. Even if they called the police, what were the police going to do? It was insane, the idea of Army guys being involved in all of this. I decided right there and then that I would find out what happened to Jacob. The semester was going to end in another month, but I didn't care. I stopped going to classes. I started researching mines, mostly abandoned mines, trying to figure out where Jacob had ended up. When he had called, he hadn't used his cell phone, so based on the caller ID, I knew he was somewhere in Nevada. The state has thousands of mines, but I managed to narrow it down to a dozen and then I hit the road."

"Do you think he's still alive?"

She shook her head slowly, avoiding his eyes again.

"How do you know for sure?"

"I just do. You know when you just know? That's how it was for me. I knew that whatever happened, Jacob had been on the run and that these people were coming for him. He wasn't going to get far. They were going to find him, and when they did, they were going to kill him."

"But you don't know for sure."

Jessica looked straight at Nova. "They killed him. I know they did. And I think I know why."

"Tell me."

"I told you, my brother was a great guy. He might have gotten into trouble in the past, but he was a great guy. I think at first he didn't know what the whole operation was. Then when he did he was, I don't know, scared at first to do anything about it. But then once he was in deep enough and understood all the ins and outs, he got the evidence he needed to go to the authorities to shut it down. And that's when they found out what he was doing and came after him."

They were quiet then, neither one speaking, both holding each other's stare. The cicadas filled the silence with their own song, a strange soothing symphony, and Jessica realized just how tired she was, how exhausted. She closed her eyes for a moment, telling herself that she was okay, that she would get through this, when she felt something crawl across her arm.

33

As the sun had set and the night had come on strong, her eyes had quickly adjusted to the dark. She could see Nova standing several yards away, the gun in his hand, just as clearly as she could see the label on the water bottle. Just as now, opening her eyes, she saw the scorpion crawling up her arm.

"Don't move."

Nova's voice, calm and steady. He began to approach her. In the sudden silence, the crunch of his shoes on the dirt was as loud as those gunshots from earlier still echoing through her head.

Jessica felt a scream rising in the back of her throat. Were scorpions poisonous? She couldn't remember. Maybe some of them were, but just how poisonous were they?

The scorpion was black and about the size of her hand. It crawled up her arm, off her skin and onto her shirt.

"It's okay," Nova said, still approaching slowly, "just sit there and don't move."

Her gaze on the scorpion, Jessica was aware of Nova stowing the gun in the waistband of his pants and then reaching into his pocket. She tried to slow her breathing. She tried to slow her heartbeat, if that was even possible. Then she heard a snick and looked up and saw Nova now holding a knife.

He held his other hand out, signaling her to remain calm. The scorpion, meanwhile, had settled on her shoulder, turning in a circle as if deciding where to go next.

Nova was close to her now, only feet away. He started to lower himself, bending at the knees, extending the blade of the knife. The scorpion turned in another circle, then started back the way it had come. Nova lowered the blade. The tip touched Jessica's skin. The scorpion paused, and for an instant she was sure it was going to strike. But then the scorpion continued forward, right onto the blade. Nova waited a beat, long enough to make sure the scorpion was balanced on the steel, and then he stood up and flung it over the rocks.

Jessica closed her eyes, released a long, deep breath.

Nova said, "You okay?"

She took another breath as she climbed to her feet. "And to think, I was worried about one of those guys killing me, not being stung by a scorpion."

"Don't worry, it wasn't poisonous," he said, but she could tell he wasn't even sure himself.

"Thank you."

He waved it away. "It was just a little bug."

"No, I mean about everything. Thank you for doing this."

"What else would I be doing? It's better than being at a crappy motel watching reruns on TV."

"What's her name?"

"Who?"

"Your girlfriend."

"I don't have a girlfriend."

"But the one you mentioned—your other team member."

"Holly?" He half-laughed. "She's not my girlfriend."

"But you care about her."

"Of course. She's my friend."

She stared at him for a long moment, studying him in the dark. "So you don't have a significant other?"

"No."

"Family?"

He shook his head.

"What about your parents?"

"My parents are dead. At least, my mom is. She died years ago, back when I was in high school. As for my old man, I hope he's dead."

"That seems harsh."

"Trust me, it isn't. When he found out my mom had cancer, he didn't stick around long. When he saw just how hard it was going to be, he split. I never heard from him since."

"That's terrible. How old were you?"

"Sixteen. He was always a hard ass. He didn't drink much, but when he did he was mean and you always had to be careful not to say the wrong thing around him. He was a mechanic and worked in one of these shops that restored vintage cars. Sometimes I went to work with him and he showed me everything he did, from taking the cars apart to putting them back together. I remember one day this Mustang came in, a 1966 Shelby GT 350, the most beautiful car I'd ever seen, and I told him I was going to own one some day. And my old man, he just laughed and said cars like that don't belong to people like us."

Nova stared off into space for a long moment, then shook his head.

"Anyway, I took care of my mom the best I could. At the time I was doing well in school, but I couldn't keep up with all the homework and tests. In the end I decided taking care of my mother was more important, so I dropped out. We didn't have insurance or enough money to get her the treatment she needed, so I started working any job I could get for whatever little money they would pay me under the table. And when I wasn't working, I was home taking care of her. We ate generic boxed spaghetti nearly every night. I see that stuff in the grocery store now and it makes my stomach roll. And the smell of Dial soap always brings back memories of washing my hands after feeding her and giving her baths. I try to avoid it the best I can, but even now, after all these years, just the scent reminds me what it was like to literally watch her shrivel to death."

Nova went quiet then, staring at her but not seeing her. She wondered what he was thinking, what awful memories were swirling through his mind. She even wanted to say something to him, apologize maybe, but he blinked and shook his head, closed the knife and slipped it back into his pocket.

"We should keep moving," he said, grabbing the canvas bag off the ground. The leather jacket had also fallen when she jumped to her feet. He picked it up and held it out to her again. "You still cold?"

She was. The jacket smelled of dirt and sweat and aftershave as she slipped it on, but it was also a safe smell, and it was warm.

"Thank you," she said again.

"Don't thank me until this is over." He handed her the canvas bag, picked up the gun she'd set on the rock and thumbed off the safety. "Now let's go."

34

The town of Kadrey was maybe half the size of Townsend, though that wasn't saying much. Townsend had a handful of fast food places, where Kadrey had none. Nova remembered driving past and barely glancing out the window. Just houses and buildings, a gas station, and that was it.

Now, in the thickening night, Kadrey hardly looked like a town at all. It was nearly eleven o'clock. The town stood dark and quiet, a few lights on inside houses, but not many. There were only a few streetlights, their bulbs as dim and fading as the stars in the sky.

Instead of heading in a direct line toward Kadrey, they had looped around to the other side, keeping a mile-wide buffer between them and the town. Connolly no doubt had men stationed on the outskirts. That was what Nova would do. Connolly had to know they would keep moving. Staying in one spot wasn't an option. Nova doubted Connolly had sent more men out looking for them, but that wasn't the point. There was only so much you could do in the desert. Nova and Jessica would need to make an escape. That meant either returning to Parrot Spur or heading toward Kadrey. Townsend wasn't an option, as the distance was just too far to make on foot, especially with Jessica's weight on his back slowing him down.

Jessica whispered, "Do you see anything?"

They lay flat on a ridge over half a mile away from town. From this angle they were facing the rear of town. A few lights on inside houses, the pulsing glow of televisions, but that was it. Between them and the houses were sagebrush and trees. The trees weren't really trees at all but overlarge bushes, maybe three dozen of them in total.

Nova concentrated on the trees. He just stared. He didn't blink. He didn't breathe. He stared and waited for any sign of movement, anything that would alert him to a sentry. Connolly's men may have once been soldiers, but that had been years ago. He doubted they kept up their training. He doubted they were still accustomed to combat situations. Their evenings were spent drinking in the bar, not lying in bed working out tactical situations in their heads.

"No," he whispered, "but that doesn't mean there's nothing there."

"You think they're out there?"

"I know they're out there. It's just a question of how many and where."

"Should we keep moving around?"

Nova thought about it. Continuing west might cost them another hour, depending on the terrain. The benefit was they would be coming up on town from a side Connolly's men wouldn't expect. Or would they? Nova wondered just how smart Connolly was. To run an operation like this, he had to be pretty smart, but right now the man was no doubt frustrated. Maybe he wasn't thinking straight. Maybe he was letting his emotions get in the way. If that was the case, maybe he wouldn't consider the idea they would loop around and approach town from the other side.

"Let's keep moving," Nova said.

Another hour passed. They took their time. Better to take their time and stay alive than to cut corners and end up dead. They had weapons, true, but Nova didn't think he could count on Jessica if it came to it. The girl was tough, but she wasn't that tough. He saw it in her eyes. He heard it in her voice.

They left the ridge and entered into rocky terrain. Nova's legs burned as they climbed up and over boulders. Then the terrain began to flatten into a copse of trees. There were many more trees than he had seen before. They seemed to border the town on this end. It didn't make sense at first, but then Nova realized these trees had been artificially placed here by the townspeople. That's the only thing that made sense. Probably decades ago some smart citizens had realized just how dangerous the rocky terrain was for kids, and so instead of putting up a wooden or wire fence, they made a natural one.

Cicadas trilled around them, masking the sound of Nova's footfalls, but still they went even slower through the trees, making sure not to disturb any branches or snap twigs.

The closer they got, the more distinct the houses became. All of them compact and no more than one story tall. Now it was midnight and most of the houses were dark and still.

Nova forced himself to keep checking the ground as they went. Good thing, too, because there was a dark pool ahead of them. He almost stepped into it when he realized it was a hole.

"What's wrong?" Jessica whispered, then looked up over his shoulder. "Are those toys down there?"

It appeared to be. Some plastic shovels and buckets in the hole, which was only a few feet wide, a few feet deep. Better kids playing outside than video games inside, Nova supposed.

They continued on. Eventually the trees and sagebrush fell away and it was just open desert between the ridge and town. This was Nova's main concern. Suddenly their cover was lost. The sky was clear and the stars were bright, but fortunately the moon wasn't full. Even a half moon would give the sentries more than enough light by which to see them. But right now it was just a sliver, and Nova hoped the sliver would allow them safe passage across the short expanse of desert.

"Hold on tight," Nova whispered.

He went faster now with the open space. The seconds seemed to last forever, and then they reached the houses.

Jessica climbed off Nova's back. Nova looked at her, asking silently if she could walk on her own. She offered up a short nod.

Most of the backyards here were fenced in, though the fences weren't tall. Nova could see over most of them. What he was looking for was an open patio door. He had to assume a town like Kadrey would have trusting neighbors. They probably locked their front doors when they went to work during the day, but their windows might be unlocked. And at night, while they slept, they might keep their patio doors open to let in the cool desert air. The only thing standing between their home and an intruder would be wire mesh.

It was the fifth house that Nova found an open patio door. Just as he hoped, a screen door was the only thing barring them entrance.

Even better, there wasn't a fence. They walked right into the backyard. There was nothing in the yard. Some white plastic patio furniture on the back porch and that was it.

Nova slung the rifle over his shoulder and withdrew his pistol in the same motion. He checked on Jessica, saw she was making decent progress, though he could tell she was in pain. She was doing her best to hide it, though, and for that he had to give her points.

They approached the patio door. Stepping up onto the concrete porch, Nova stared through the screen door at the darkness beyond. Suddenly he wondered if this was a trap. If Connolly was even smarter than Nova had thought. If Connolly had known exactly what Nova was going to do even before Nova did. If at this moment one of Connolly's men—if not Connolly himself—stood just beyond that screen door, an Uzi aimed for center mass.

Nova got closer. Peered inside. An empty kitchen. Table and chairs, counter, sink, stove, refrigerator. And on the wall, snug in its cradle, was a phone.

Predictably, the screen door was locked. Nova wouldn't have wanted it any other way. Had it been unlocked, warning bells would have gone off inside his head.

He used his knife to slice an X beside the handle. The X was large enough for him to stick his hand through. A twist of the wrist, a flick of the lock, and the screen door was open.

Nova checked on Jessica standing beside him as he took hold of the handle. He held his breath, waited a beat, then began to slide it open. It made some noise but the noise was slight, almost drowned out by the cicadas. He slid the door just far enough that Jessica could slip through, then himself, and pushed it closed again.

They stood silent then, listening to the house. A clock ticked somewhere in another room. The refrigerator hummed. The scent of dinner lingered. In the trashcan beside the refrigerator was an empty Hungry-Man frozen meal box.

Nova headed directly for the phone. He pulled the phone from its cradle and placed it to his ear. The dial tone was the sweetest sound he had heard all night. Before he had left D.C., Atticus had given him a business card with a number on it. Atticus had said that if Nova ever needed anything to give the number a call. Nova had memorized the number before burning the business card. He hadn't thought he would ever need to use the number but wanted to be safe rather than sorry. Now he was glad he hadn't dismissed it.

He set the phone against his shoulder and started pressing buttons. It was a long distance call, and he had only gotten through five digits when Jessica sucked in air through her teeth. He tilted his face in her direction, saw her staring past him, fear in her eyes.

The kitchen light turned on.

35

Nova spun fast, raising his pistol, but immediately paused when he saw the man standing there.

He was an older man, sixties or seventies, black with a weathered face and gray hair and beard. He wore a stained undershirt, his gut hanging out over a baggy pair of jeans. In his hands was a rifle, and it was the rifle that made Nova pause. Not because it was currently aimed toward the floor, but because it was so old.

Not quite an antique, it looked like a Browning that hadn't been used in over fifty years. Had it been anything modern, some kind of assault rifle, Nova would have placed a bullet between the old man's eyes and asked questions later. Because Connolly's men, from what Nova had seen, only had the newest artillery. But this rifle? This looked like the kind of rifle the old man's father had once used to go hunting.

Nova lowered the gun to his side. He whispered, "Mind turning off the light?"

The old man said nothing. He stared at Nova with dark eyes. He kept the rifle aimed toward the floor.

"We apologize for trespassing, but we're not here to hurt you. We're not here to steal anything from you. We just need to use your phone."

The old man's eyes shifted from Nova to Jessica, then back to Nova. Still he said nothing.

"Some men are trying to hurt us. We just need to call for help. That's all. You let me make the call, then we'll be on our way and out of your hair. But first, please turn off the light. We don't want to alert these men that we're here."

The man stood motionless for a long time, his gaze steady on Nova. Then, keeping the rifle aimed toward the floor with his right hand, he lifted his left hand and flicked the switch on the wall. The kitchen light when off.

"Thank you," Nova whispered.

The man said nothing. Nova's night vision had momentarily been displaced because of the light, but he saw what he thought was the man making a slight nod.

Nova turned back to the phone. It had disconnected and was beeping. He fingered the button to restart it and again heard the dial tone. He glanced once more at the old man who kept motionless and quiet, the rifle aimed toward the floor, then dialed. The phone rang once, twice, three times. Then there was a click and a woman's voice.

"Thank you for calling Scout Dry Cleaners. Our normal business hours are Monday through Friday, seven a.m to seven p.m., and on Saturday eight a.m. to three p.m. We are closed Sundays."

Nova stared at the dial pad. Had he remembered the number wrong? Had he punched it in wrong? Had Atticus given him the wrong—

Wait. Scout Dry Cleaners. Atticus. Was that the hint, a *To Kill a Mockingbird* reference?

A lengthy number of seconds passed in silence, and then a beep sounded.

Nova hesitated a moment, then said, "This is Nova. I stumbled across an operation cooking meth in an abandoned mine in Parrot Spur, Nevada. They're after me and a civilian." He paused. "The men are ex-military. They're the real deal. We don't have much time."

He replaced the phone in its cradle. Turned toward Jessica who was watching him with big eyes. Then he turned back to the old man.

"Thank you."

Now that his eyes had adjusted again to the dark, Nova watched the old man nod slightly.

"We'll be going now. I cut your screen door. I'll pay for the damages later, if that's okay with you."

The man nodded again.

Nova motioned Jessica toward the door. She started across the kitchen, Nova behind her. Abruptly she stopped. Nova almost walked into her, looked past her through the screen door at the backyard. He saw exactly what she saw. The moon was only a sliver, but it was just enough to see two shadowy figures crossing the yard, assault rifles at the ready, taking up position.

Nova took Jessica's arm and pulled her back. He looked around the house. Probably two bedrooms, a bathroom, a living room, maybe a TV room. The door off to the right led into the garage. Nowhere safe to take cover.

He watched the two figures out in the backyard make their approach. He remembered making his approach only minutes ago, staring through the screen door at the darkness beyond. He had imagined one of Connolly's men inside, an Uzi aimed for center mass. He hadn't been certain the kitchen was empty until he was right up on the patio. Which meant the two men in the backyard couldn't see him, at least not yet, which gave Nova an advantage.

Pocketing the gun, he slipped the rifle off his shoulder and moved to a better position. The space between him and the screen door was maybe ten feet. He crouched and aimed, hoping for the men to suddenly turn around and walk away. Maybe they were just searching all the yards. Maybe this was a coincidence. But Nova knew that wasn't the case. The old man had turned on the kitchen light. Connolly's men were probably stationed all around town, watching for something strange to happen. The light coming on may not have immediately signaled that it was their quarry, but still it was enough to bring the men here. And if two men were in the backyard, it was safe to assume there were more men out front. Boxing them in. Decreasing their chances of survival with every second that ticked off the clock in the next room.

Nova thumbed off the safety. He fingered the trigger, watching the closest shadowy figure. He waited a beat, then squeezed the trigger, shifted the rifle a quarter inch, and squeezed the trigger again. Both men dropped to the ground. Neither one moved.

He surveyed the rest of the backyard. No movement. He stood back up and turned toward Jessica and the old man. Even in the dark he saw the shock on the old man's face.

"I'm sorry," Nova said.

That was when the front door burst open.

36

Two men came in heavy, decked out in full assault gear, strapped with AR-15s. They had a direct bead on the old man, and when the old man turned, bringing up the rifle, the men didn't hesitate—they opened fire.

Nova pushed Jessica to the floor. He dove over the kitchen table into the living room. Rolling onto the carpet, tipping over an end table, he came back up and took out the first man, then the second. The second man's finger was stuck on the trigger, and he sprayed bullets at the ceiling as he went down, chunks of plaster falling like rain.

"Are you okay?" he asked Jessica.

She was slowly picking herself up off the floor, grimacing at the pain in her ankle. "I think so."

Nova approached the men, slowly, knowing the first man was dead, the second man still alive. That man was on the floor, taking quick, shallow breaths, blood around his mouth. His eyes shifted up to meet Nova.

Nova checked the broken front door. Through it was a narrow walkway that led to the street. The street itself was deserted, the houses beyond it dark and quiet.

He crouched down beside the man. "How many others are there?"

The man glared up at Nova.

A gasp drew Nova's attention. Jessica was now in the hallway on her knees beside the old man. He had been shot repeatedly in the chest. His undershirt was soaked with blood.

Jessica looked at Nova, tears brimming her eyes. "He's dead."

Nova withdrew his knife. The blade popped up, the handle whirled in his hand, and suddenly the knife was in the man's thigh.

The man grunted in pain, blinked several times, but said nothing.

"How many?"

When the man still said nothing, Nova twisted the knife.

The man grunted again, his breaths quickening even more.

"Stop it!" Jessica shouted. "Haven't enough people died already?"

Nova kept his focus on the man glaring back at him.

"Not even close."

He pulled out the knife, spun the handle again, and shoved the blade into the man's throat.

Outside, the growing roar of engines filled the night. Nova left the blade in the man's throat. He grabbed his rifle and stood back up. He approached one of the windows, using the barrel of the rifle to move the curtain. Two pickup trucks, both with heightened suspension, screeched to a halt in front of the house. Doors opened and men piled out. There were five of them in all, fanning out across the lawn. They didn't advance, but they kept their positions, all aiming rifles at the house.

An SUV arrived. The passenger door opened and out stepped Connolly. He wore full assault gear, just like the rest of the men, only his hand was bandaged. In his other hand he held a radio. He placed the radio to his mouth, began to talk. Nova could hear his voice outside, but he could also hear a faint whispering coming from behind him. He turned, confused at first, then noticed the comm units in both of the dead men's ears.

Each comm unit wrapped around the ear, its connecting wire disappearing beneath their vests and coming out to the radios clipped to their belts. Nova moved to the first dead man, stripped him of the earpiece and radio, clipped the radio to his own belt and put the earpiece in his ear.

Moving back to the window, hitting the toggle switch, Nova said, "Is the job offer still on the table?"

"Casanova Bartkowski," Connolly said. "Am I pronouncing that right? Just who the fuck names their kid Casanova?"

"How's the hand?"

"You are quite an anomaly. We got your name from your car, but that wasn't even your real name. It took a while to crack your false ID, then I had a friend of mine search your name through the Pentagon. Like you said, you were a SEAL. Served quite a few tours. Impressive. But then a few years ago your record goes black. My friend had never seen that before, so he did more digging. Not even five minutes passed before he got a phone call from someone way up the chain asking him what the fuck he thought he was doing. Scared the shit out of him, is what he told me."

"It sounds like your friend is a pussy."

"You're surrounded. I have men out back, too. You might as well give up now and save us all some time."

"The man who owns this house is dead."

"I'm sorry to hear that."

"He had nothing to do with any of this."

"That's true. But you brought this fight to his doorstep—literally. Don't blame me."

Across the street a few lights came on. Curtains moved, faces peeked out, then those faces disappeared and the lights went off.

Connolly said, "Do you think anyone in this town is going to help you? I own them all. I own the police. I can do whatever the fuck I want. Now put down your weapons and come out with the girl."

Nova returned to the two dead men. He shouldered their AR-15s and moved into the kitchen to check the window over the sink. Three men were fanned out in the backyard.

Hitting the toggle switch again, he said, "I have a counter offer."

Amusement in Connolly's voice: "And what is that?"

Nova checked the garage, found only the outline of a car in the darkness, a propane gas grill beside the door, then started toward the other end of the house to check the other rooms. "You and your men get back in the trucks and leave. I'll give you an hour head start."

"Before what?"

"Before I track down and kill every last one of your men. I'll save you for last."

The amusement didn't leave Connolly's voice. "You're delusional."

"No, I'm pissed. There's a difference."

"Very well. I'll give you ten more seconds until my men open fire."

Nothing useful in the bedroom or bathroom, at least at a second's glance.

"Ten."

Nova hurried back down the hallway.

"Nine."

He passed Jessica, dropping the two AR-15s on the carpet beside her, and went straight for the garage door.

"Eight."

Yanked the propane tank from the grill.

"Seven."

The tank didn't want to come at first, and he had to jiggle a lever in the back to get it to pop out.

"Six."

Took the tank to the refrigerator.

"Five."

Opened the door, the light coming on inside, illuminating soda and cold cuts and ketchup and mayonnaise, and he swept it all out onto the floor, along with the middle panel.

"Four."

Shoved the propane tank inside, slammed the door shut.

"Three."

Hurried back to Jessica still on her knees beside the dead old man, now openly sobbing.

"Two."

He fell down beside her, whispered into her ear, "Just stay flat and don't move," and pushed her down onto the carpet, covering her with his body.

"One."

37

The AR-15s he took off the two dead men were Colt Competition CRP-18s. A match-grade, air-gauged, polished 416 stainless steel 18-inch custom barrel. A triple-port muzzle brake. Guaranteed accuracy of one inch or less for a three-shot group at one hundred yards. A .223 Remington caliber with a 30-round magazine.

Nova had to assume the men outside were carrying the same hardware. Which meant with five men in front and three men out back, that was 240 rounds.

The onslaught lasted only ten seconds. Nova was counting them down in his head, while Jessica trembled and screamed beneath him. While glass and plaster and all bits and pieces of the house splintered and flew everywhere.

Ten seconds, over 200 rounds, and then that was it. A sudden lull. Silence and the echo of gunfire.

In his ear, Connolly asked, "Still alive in there?"

Nova pushed away from Jessica. She had her eyes closed. "Are you okay?"

She looked up at him, nodded quickly. He jumped to his

feet and started toward the refrigerator, trampling over bits of plaster and glass. Glanced through the shattered window over the sink and saw the men in the backyard reloading their rifles.

Connolly said, "We can keep doing this all night. We have more ammunition than we know what to do with. Come on, Bartkowski, can you hear me?"

Nova opened the fridge door and the light came on inside, briefly spotlighting the destruction of the kitchen. He pulled the propane tank out and slammed the door shut.

"Bartkowski, talk to me. You ready to surrender yet?"

Nova crossed the kitchen toward the living room, the propane tank at his side, hitting the radio's toggle switch again.

"Yeah, we're coming out now."

He adjusted the tank so it lay in the palm of his hand, his other hand on top. It wasn't nearly as heavy as he would have liked it to be, and he had no idea just how much propane was inside, but he hoped it was enough.

Behind him, Jessica whispered, "What are you doing?"

He paused just a few feet away from the broken front door. The windows had been shattered, the curtains destroyed, the place looking like it was ready for the demolition crew.

"Grab those two rifles and get ready to run out the back."

He kept moving forward, swinging his arm back underhanded like the propane tank was a bowling ball, because really that's what it felt like now, like he was bowling and the pickup trucks and men in the street were just pins waiting to be knocked over. Then, before he knew it, the tank was no longer in his hand. Now it was flying through the air, hitting the walkway, bouncing and continuing to roll toward the street. It wobbled for a second and Nova worried it would stop completely, but it kept going, the men all tracking it with their rifles, seemingly hypnotized, Connolly standing on the other side of the vehicles, the radio in his hand, confusion on his face. But the confusion only lasted an instant before realization started to build, and by then Nova had his pistol in hand, aimed at the rolling propane tank, waiting for just the right moment to squeeze the trigger.

Connolly shouted, "Everyone get down!"

Nova squeezed the trigger.

The explosion wasn't nearly as massive as Nova had hoped for, but it was still large enough to light up the front yard and bark a hectic *whoosh*. One of the pickup trucks tipped over onto its side. Men close by were thrown back, and several car alarms nearby began to blare. Nova didn't have time to see what other destruction it caused, because by then he was rushing back through the house, motioning at Jessica to follow him. The girl looked helpless in the dark, completely lost, her eyes wide as she stared out through the broken front door.

"Jessica!"

She blinked, the spell of the fire outside broken, and turned her head in his direction. He took one of the AR-15s from her, told her to sling the other one over her shoulder. She nodded and started limping toward him as he ran for the screen door. The thing was now in tatters. The rifle at the ready, he opened fire the moment he stepped outside.

He took the man closest to him out first, then the second man only yards away. The third moved off to the right, firing blindly, and Nova had to dive down into the grass. The rifle was spent and he didn't have time to load a new magazine, so he pulled his gun out and returned fire. One of the bullets struck the man in the leg, sent him to the ground. Nova, back on his feet, closed the distance between him and the man. The man started to bring up his rifle but then paused, pain all over his face.

Nova hesitated. For a moment he saw the man there on the ground not as a soldier in Connolly's army but just another human being, a guy who might have a family. Then the image of the old man dead on the floor, his undershirt crimson with blood, filled his mind.

He placed a bullet in the man's head.

Movement behind him, and Nova spun around, his gun raised, finger on the trigger.

Jessica stared back at him, her eyes still wide, just outside the tattered screen door.

"Here," Nova said, lowering the gun to his side and hurrying forward. He turned and bent and scooped her up onto his back, just like they had done before, the move almost familiar now between the two of them despite the fact they had just started doing it hours ago. Then Nova was running, Jessica on his back, away from the house toward the desert.

On the other side of the house the car alarms kept blaring. The men out front kept shouting. Somewhere nearby a dog barked.

They just needed to reach the trees. That was it. Once they reached the trees, they would be okay. They could hide, disappear, wait it out until Atticus sent help—*if* Atticus sent help. The possibility that the phone number wasn't the right number kept playing in the back of Nova's mind, but he refused to accept it. If that was the case, then they were dead.

Nova had never gone this fast with Jessica on his back. It was difficult to say who was having the harder time, but halfway to the trees, Jessica's grip on him began to loosen. By the time he sensed it and tried to stop it, it was already too late. She fell away, first her grip, then her entire body.

Jessica hit the ground hard, landing on her sprained ankle. She cried out in pain. Nova dug his heels into the dirt, spun back around, and saw her there in the grass, maybe fifty yards away. How she had managed to fall back so far, he couldn't say, but it was what was beyond her that worried him. Men were coming—at least a half dozen—running full out. They would be here any second.

The men were just vague figures in the dark, but Nova fired at them anyway. The men were spread out and running fast and none of the bullets hit a mark, at least none that were apparent to Nova. Then the slide kicked back and Nova was reaching for a fresh magazine when he realized he didn't have one. He started to reach for the rifle strapped over his shoulder when he remembered that he had exhausted its ammunition back at the house and didn't have an extra magazine, either. Jessica had the other AR-15, and she was right there, only fifty yards away.

He started forward when the men opened fire. The ground around him kicked up dirt. Bullets whizzed by him. Nova tried to make himself as small as possible, his heart rate up, his whole body on edge, debating what the right thing was to do. The dark figures became whole as headlights appeared behind them. One of the pickup trucks had squeezed between two of the houses and was headed in their direction.

Nova glanced once again at Jessica on the ground. Only fifty yards away, yet it seemed a mile. She gave him a look—a plain, simple look—and then before he knew it he was running. Not toward her, like he wanted, but away, toward the supposed safety of the trees, completely weaponless, bullets flying at his back.

38

The men were on her at once. They grabbed her arms and yanked her to her feet. The rifle strap had twisted around her arm, and one of the men tried to repeatedly tug it off, Jessica screaming in pain, before another man told the other man to stop. They held her in place for a beat, just long enough to un-thread the strap from her arm, and then the rifle was gone and they were pushing her forward, toward the houses.

Jessica only went a few feet before her ankle gave out and she fell to the ground.

"Shit," said one of the men.

"Now what?" asked another man.

Hands grabbed at her again, picking her up, and next thing Jessica knew she was flipped over someone's shoulder, the man carrying her fireman-style.

Part of her wanted to struggle, wanted to shout, wanted to do whatever she could do get this man to release her, but then what? It wasn't like she could do much on her own. She could barely walk more than a few steps without grimacing in pain. Even if she had a weapon, could she really bring herself to shoot these men? Maybe. But even so, she doubted any of her bullets would hit their mark.

She was aware of more men racing past them toward the trees. That pickup truck kept going too, its headlights burning a path in the dark. The man carrying her said, "I got her," and Jessica wasn't sure who he was talking to at first, as there was nobody near them, but then came a faint, distant whisper from the man's ear: "Good."

Through the backyard, past the dead men, around the house, and into the front yard—Jessica watched it all from the perspective of leaving it behind. Then the man stopped, took her off his shoulder, and set her down on the ground. They were in the street, right in front of the dead man's house, beside an SUV and pickup truck. The pickup truck lay on its side, its windows shattered.

Connolly approached her, his eyes full of rage, and grabbed the bottom of her face to force her to look at him.

"You're a bigger pain in the ass than your brother." Her pushed her away, said, "Put her in the truck."

The man opened the back door and pushed her inside, forced her to slide across the seat so he could climb up in after her. Connolly and his assistant got into the SUV, Connolly behind the wheel, his assistant in the passenger seat.

Connolly started the engine, let it idle for a couple of seconds, then placed the radio to his mouth.

"Bartkowski, can you hear me?"

Silence.

"Bartkowski, I have the girl. If you want to save her, surrender yourself immediately."

Silence.

Connolly shifted in his seat, turned and extended the radio back toward Jessica. He said to the man beside her, "Kick her ankle."

"What?"

"Kick her fucking ankle!"

The man's kick wasn't very hard, but still it was enough to cause her to scream in pain.

Smiling, Connolly said into the radio, "Did you hear that, Bartkowski? We can do this all night."

Silence.

The assistant said, "Maybe he can't hear you."

"He can hear me."

"But what if he can't?"

The radio crackled, but it wasn't Nova's voice that spoke.

"Sir, we have a problem."

"What is it?"

"The truck's losing gas. Looks like the tank got hit during the explosion. Permission to take it back to town before it loses all fuel."

Connolly didn't speak for a long moment. Despite the fact his back was to her, Jessica could tell he was seething. In the glow of the dash she could see the radio shaking in his hand.

"Fine," he said. "But let's get more men out there immediately. Any luck yet?"

"Not yet, sir."

"Find him."

Connolly tossed the radio to his assistant, revved the engine again, and glanced back at her. "You want to see what's inside the mine so badly? Okay, I'll show you. I'll show you exactly what got your brother killed."

39

"Find him," Connolly said, but there was no answer. Nova hadn't expected one. He was surprised the men had stayed on this channel in the first place, though maybe the men didn't care that he could hear what they were planning. Only it wasn't like there was much of a plan. Currently they were playing a game of cat and mouse, and Nova was the mouse. Except he was a smart mouse.

Even from where he hid, he smelled the gasoline. After all, the truck stood maybe thirty yards away. The driver got down on his knees again, shining the flashlight at the undercarriage once more.

"Motherfucker," he mumbled.

Ahead of Nova, through the trees, the other men continued forward. They had given up any pretense of stealth, and branches and twigs snapped like firecrackers. They had turned on their flashlights, too, and white beams of light sliced through the night.

Nova didn't move. He didn't breathe. But that didn't mean his blood wasn't boiling. He hadn't given into Connolly's attempt to goad him, but that didn't mean Nova wasn't fucking pissed. In his earpiece he could still hear an echo of Jessica's screams.

It had hit him the moment he burst through the copse of trees. The men chasing him expected him to go forward. So instead, Nova had gone backward. Right into that hole he had almost stepped in less than an hour ago, the one with the children's toys. He dropped down and threw clumps of loose dirt on himself to mute his gray T-shirt. And the men had hurried past, adrenaline and velocity and Connolly breathing down their necks forcing them forward. Then, behind those men, the pickup pulled to a stop and the driver jumped out and realized the gas tank was leaking.

Now the driver started to get back in the pickup. Nova thought about charging the man. It was maybe thirty yards between him and the truck. From this angle he could slip into the passenger seat before the man put the truck in gear. Assuming, of course, the passenger-side door was unlocked. Once inside the cab, he could overpower the man. Punch him in his windpipe, disable him long enough to strip him of any weapon he currently carried. He could then take the pickup and go after Connolly.

Only he didn't know where Connolly was headed. Nova had an idea where he was headed, but without confirmation, he would be showing his hand, when right now his best bet was to stay far below the radar.

So as the pickup's engine roared to life once again, Nova did something that surprised even himself: He tore out of the hole, charged toward the pickup, dropped to the ground, rolled under the truck, and reached for whatever he could find.

It was too dark to see, and the stench of gasoline was overpowering, but the pickup had heightened suspension and gave him more than enough room. First he found one solid handgrip, then another, then came the real struggle: something to do with his feet. By then the driver was putting the truck in gear. In the next second the truck would begin moving. Nova lifted his right foot, then his left foot, searching for anyplace to keep them. The truck began to reverse, and his left foot found a hold, then his right foot. It wasn't ideal but it would work for now. Nova just hoped he could hold on the entire way back to Parrot Spur.

40

The pickup was a Ford Super Duty F-250. Its V8 engine roared as it tore across the grass, slowing briefly to squeeze between two houses, and then accelerated over the sidewalk into the street.

Nova couldn't tell whether it was because of sweat or grease, but his right hand began to slip. He kept squeezing it, trying to regain a steady grip, while also keeping his other hand and feet secure. He knew the risks. He knew what would happen if he fell. His head smacking off the macadam at such a speed wasn't nearly as bad as being run over by the truck's massive rear tires.

The pickup slowed as it came to the stop sign right before the highway—but then accelerated immediately, its rear tires squealing as its fishtailed and streaked lines of rubber.

Nova's right hand slipped from the sudden jerk. His fingers scraped against the highway. His head started to fall back. He could feel the highway right beneath him, begging him to let go.

But he didn't. He braced himself and pushed his hand back up, searching for the hold he had before. He found it, but his fingers began to slip again. Bracing himself once more, he wiped his hand on his pants then reached for the hold again. This time his fingers stayed in place.

Every muscle in his body straining, Nova closed his eyes, took a deep breath, and waited.

He didn't have to wait long.

The distance between Kadrey and Parrot Spur was only eight miles. The highway was empty at this time of night, and even if it wasn't, the driver wasn't one to care. His boss apparently owned this entire area of the state. No cops were going to pull him over for speeding, so the driver drove with a lead foot.

At some point they passed the entrance to the mine. Nova was aware of it just as he was aware that Jessica might be there right now.

Eventually the truck's speed began to taper. The engine's roar lessened.

Nova wanted to look where they were exactly, but he didn't want to lower his head. If he lowered it too far, his skull might connect with the highway, and that was not something he wanted to try. So he waited, braced against the undercarriage, as the truck slowed. It turned left, meaning it was headed for the bar and diner and motel side of the highway. It didn't park in front of the bar, however, and instead moved around to the back.

Finally the truck came to a full stop. Its engine growled for another couple of seconds, then went silent.

Certain the truck wasn't going to move again, Nova lowered himself to the ground. He lay there for a moment, relishing the feel of solid ground, then heard the driver shifting around in his seat.

The pickup truck's door opened. Its suspension squeaked. First one foot appeared on the ground only inches away from Nova, then the second.

Before the man even had a chance to take one full step, Nova reached out and grabbed the man's ankles. He yanked back and pushed up. The man grunted a shout of surprise as he fell. He managed to get his hands up to soften the fall, but that didn't matter. By then Nova rolled out from under the truck, rose to a knee, and punched the man in the face. The man turned over, reached for his gun, but Nova punched him again. Then he leaned forward and hooked an arm around the man's throat. He positioned himself right behind the man and applied pressure. The man struggled, his arms and legs flaying, but as the seconds ticked by, the struggling began to diminish.

Nova set the now unconscious man aside and got to his feet. He searched the man's pockets. A gun and a knife, two spare magazines, and that was it. He checked the truck, opening the door as soundlessly as he could, and rummaged through the glove box until he found what he was looking for. Stepping back, he rolled the man over so he was lying right beneath the truck on his belly. He drew the man's left arm back, then his right arm, and secured his wrists on the other end of the cab step with the zip-tie. He wished he had something to put over the man's mouth in case he came to, but there was nothing else. It didn't matter anyway; Nova doubted there was anybody in town. All the men had been dispatched to Kadrey and the surrounding desert to search for him.

Where they would be looking for a very long time, he thought, and smiled.

Now what he needed was a vehicle. And weapons. As many weapons as he could get his hands on.

He started toward the side of the bar when he heard the crunch of gravel. Nova paused, listening closely, and determined it was two sets of footsteps.

"Are you sure it was him?" said a voice, the tone natural and calm, not at all concerned about being heard.

"Yeah, I saw him pull in," said the other voice. Then, calling out: "Greg, you back there?"

Greg, of course, didn't answer.

"See," said the first voice, "I told you it wasn't him."

"It's him."

Nova withdrew the gun from his waistband. He dropped the magazine into his hand, checked the number of rounds, then slid it back in as quietly as possible.

The crunch of gravel was very close now, right around the corner.

The same man as before called, "Hey, Greg, what's the hold up?"

The men turned the corner and stopped abruptly. They stared at the barrel of Nova's gun. One of the men went to grab for his weapon.

"Don't," Nova said.

The man paused.

Nova said, "I did your friend over there a favor by not ending his life. I don't have to end your lives either, but that all depends on you. Now put your hands on top of your heads."

Neither man moved. Neither spoke.

"I should save myself time and hassle and kill you both, but I'm trying to be a nice guy. Now put your hands on top of your heads."

One of the men glanced at his friend, and shrugged. "Why not?"

Suddenly both men fell away from each other, widening the gap between them. It was an expert move, one Nova would no doubt have used, and it was because of that he was ready for it.

The men went for their guns. Nova shot the one on the right in the throat, and then spun away as the other man fired at him. He fell to a knee, aimed, and shot the other man right in his face.

Nova was quiet for a moment, listening to the night around him. Past the cicadas in the desert to any other sounds that might alert him to approaching danger.

He dropped the magazine again into his hand. The light was faint, but it was enough to see only two rounds left. He tossed the magazine to the ground, went to reach for the full one in his pocket, when gravel crunched behind him.

Nova didn't even bother turning around. Not fully at least. He simply tilted his head, just enough to watch Nancy Price step out of the shadows, a shotgun in her hands. When she spoke, her nicotine-laced voice was steady and strong.

"Drop it or I'll blow your head off."

41

Because of her ankle, the man dragged her through the tunnel. Connolly and his assistant walked ahead of them, Connolly silent and sullen, a gun in his hand.

Eventually they came to a door. This struck Jessica as odd, though she wasn't sure why that should be. This whole thing was odd. After all, she knew what was inside this mine—or at least had a good idea—so it shouldn't have surprised her at all.

A keypad was on the door by the handle. The assistant went to punch in the code, but paused when Connolly placed a hand on his arm.

Glancing back at her, Connolly said, "I always knew I wanted to do something with this mine. I grew up in Townsend, you understand. Every day I saw the smoke coming from the factory, and every day I promised myself I wouldn't end up working there like my old man. That's why I ended up going into the military. It was my way of escape. My way of making something of myself."

"Be all you can be," Jessica said. "Is that it?"

"You have no idea what it's like to serve your country, being fed a bunch of bullshit, and then realizing there isn't anything for you on the outside, what you consider normal life. I knew men who had found 'normal' jobs, but they weren't happy. They could barely pay the bills. The system fucked them over, so I figured, why not fuck the system over. I found the right contacts, the right backers, and I did something very few men who come out of the service manage to do."

"What's that?"

"I created an empire."

He nodded at his assistant, who punched in the code and pushed open the door. The assistant held the door open for Connolly and the man dragging Jessica.

It was dark at first, but then the assistant flipped a switch and lights began to wink on, one after another, until the darkness was chased completely away.

"When they started digging this mine," Connolly said, leading them down an incline, "no one could have possibly known this cavern was here. But the miners didn't care. They just kept digging. It wasn't until fifty years later someone was smart enough to see its potential."

The cavern wasn't very large, about the size of a small movie theater. The jagged ceiling was maybe forty feet high. In the middle of the cavern sat a steel room. It reminded Jessica of the shed her parents had out behind the house, only this was much bigger. One hundred feet long, thirty feet wide. There were enough windows on the room that Jessica would see all the equipment inside. Large industrial equipment, numerous pipes and tubing. On the other side of the room several pipes snaked toward and disappeared into the darkness of the cavern.

"Despite the fact I pretty much own Parrot Spur and Kadrey, it's not like I can manufacture drugs out in the open. I may be arrogant, but I'm not stupid. At first we manufactured cocaine, but there were distribution problems with getting the right supplies, and then the market for coke started petering out. What began to rise up in its place was methamphetamine. Our chemists churn out over two hundred pounds of product every week. It's some of the best product in the country, if not the very best."

Connolly led them down a short walkway toward a long steel table beside the room. There were a handful of rolling chairs tucked underneath. He pulled one out, spun it around, and pushed it toward her.

The man threw her down on the chair. He stood back, crossing his arms, and leaned against the table. The assistant stood off to the side, his hands folded in front of him. Connolly pulled out another chair and rolled it so it faced her. He sat down, took a deep breath, and crossed his leg over his knee.

"So," he said.

Jessica glared back at him. "Are you going to kill me?"

"Probably."

"Why not get it over with?"

"Because right now you are what is considered an asset. Bartkowski has already come all this way to try to keep you safe. He's not just going to let you go. If my men don't find him, he'll come and try to find you."

"How will he know I'm here?"

"He'll know. It's the most obvious place."

"And then what—you're going to kill us both?"

Connolly didn't even crack a grin, his gaze level with hers. "That's right."

"Just like you killed my brother."

Now Connolly did smile, shaking his head slowly. "You have it all wrong."

"What do you mean?"

"All this time you've, what, thought of your brother as a

hero? As a good guy fighting against drug addiction in our country?" He snorted a laugh. "You have no fucking clue."

"You may not have killed my brother yourself, but your men did."

"No, Jessica, I'm afraid that's not the case. My men didn't kill your brother. Your brother killed himself."

42

"Get down on your knees."

Nova didn't move. "You don't want to do this."

The barrel of the shotgun barely even wavered. Nancy Price's face was impassive. "Get down. On your. Knees."

"How did you get mixed up in this mess anyway?"

"Not that it's any of your business, but I've been in this town ever since I was a girl. Grew up across the highway in one of those houses, worked at the diner, then at the bar. Now I own the bar, thanks to Mr. Connolly."

"How generous of him."

"I knew from the moment you walked into my bar you were trouble."

"I think that's a line from a country song."

"Shut up. I don't need to hear you talk. We had a good thing going until you and that bitch came along."

"Actually, you want to blame anybody, you should blame that sniper of yours. He's the one who blew my tires. If it wasn't for him, I'd already be in California by now."

"Yeah, and now he's dead. You killed him."

Nova shrugged. "His death was more of an accident, to tell you the truth."

"Joe was a good friend of mine. All the men who've died to-day were good friends of mine. And they're all dead, no thanks to you."

Nancy adjusted the butt of the shotgun on her shoulder. Even in the faint light Nova felt her glare burn into him.

"Get on your knees," she said. "I'm not going to tell you again."

"These friends of yours killed an old man. He was just mind-ing his own business, and they shot him to death, destroyed his house."

Nancy grunted. "Why should I give a shit about some old nigger?"

So apparently she knew all about it. Probably even knew the old man's name, but instead wanted to refer to him as a nigger.

Nova said, "I'm sorry you feel that way, Nancy."

"How so? I'm the one holding a shotgun on you."

"Yeah, and my friend is currently holding his gun on you," Nova said, tilting his head at the pickup truck behind her.

She didn't even blink. Instead, she smiled. "Nice try. I might have been born at night, but I wasn't born last night."

Nova looked past her, his gaze intent on an invisible person. "Shoot her."

Nancy tilted the shotgun so the barrel was pointed at Nova's legs. "I'll shoot you."

Well shit, Nova thought, now what was he supposed to do?

As it turned out, the invisible person behind Nancy made the first move. Sort of. Yes, Nova had been hoping that the old woman would fall for a trick designed to fool a child. It hadn't worked, because Nancy knew better. But when Greg, the driver of the F-250, began to come to, he moaned, and it was this sudden noise that startled Nancy. It drew her attention, only for a moment, but a moment was all Nova needed.

He charged forward, sidestepping the barrel of the shotgun, and shoved it up toward the sky. Nancy pulled the trigger. The shotgun exploded. Nancy tried to bring it back down, but Nova easily wrestled it out of her hands. Now with the weapon in his possession, he swung the shotgun back so the butt connected with Nancy's forehead.

She went down but did not lose consciousness. Blood began soaking into her hair.

Nova went to take a step toward her when headlights swept the parking lot. He froze, listening to the tires grinding the gravel and Greg still groaning underneath the pickup truck.

The vehicle parked. The engine went silent. A door opened. Nancy moaned.

Nova heard footsteps on the gravel, coming quickly toward the rear of the building. He slid up next to the wall, waiting, until a gun appeared around the corner. Nova waited another moment, the shotgun in his hands, then dropped the weapon and stepped forward and grabbed the hands holding the gun. Those hands belonged to Sheriff Leonard Smith. The old man grunted in surprise as Nova whirled him into the wall. The back of his head smacked against the concrete. Just as quickly the gun was then in Nova's hand, aimed at the sheriff.

"Fancy seeing you here," Nova said, pushing the barrel of the gun into the sheriff's neck. "Where's the girl?"

The fear he had expected to see in Nancy's eyes materialized in the sheriff's. His body shaking, his eyes wide, he said, "The mine. She's at the mine."

"How many men are there?"

"Not many. Two or three."

Holding the sheriff against the wall, Nova peeked around the corner at the Crown Vic parked in front of the bar's entrance.

"I'll tell you anything you want," the sheriff said. His wide gaze skipped around the bodies around them, first at the two dead men, then at Nancy and Greg. "Just don't kill me."

It wasn't an act. Nova had expected better of the sheriff, but he could see the fear in the old man's eyes. He wouldn't be surprised if a piss stain soon appeared on the sheriff's trousers.

"Don't," Nancy moaned from her place on the ground. "Your nephew ... will kill you."

"Shut up," Nova said to Nancy. Then to the sheriff: "Your nephew?"

The old man kept looking around at the bodies, trembling even more.

"Do you know where my Mustang is?"

The old man nodded quickly.

Nova took the gun away just a few inches, the barrel's indentation showing in the man's skin. "Then why don't you tell me where it is. And while you do that, Sheriff, take off your clothes."

The old man's bottom lip quivered. "W-W-W-Why?"

Nova pressed the barrel of the gun between the sheriff's eyes. "Because I don't want to get any blood on them."

43

Connolly leaned forward in the chair, studying Jessica's face. He waited for her to speak, and when she didn't, he said, "You want to cry. I can see it in your eyes. Don't hold them back on my account."

Jessica didn't want to give him the satisfaction of seeing her shed any tears. Still, she didn't have that much control over it, and she could feel her eyes starting to water no matter how hard she tried to stop them.

The assistant stood quietly off to the side, the man who had dragged her stood quietly behind her, and Jessica sat in the chair, glaring back at Connolly as he smiled at her.

"You're lying." She had to force the words out, doing everything she could to hide the tremor in her voice.

"I figured you would say that. It's pure denial. You don't want to accept the truth about your brother, that's understandable. You grew up—where was it—just outside of Detroit? Certainly not the most prosperous place, especially after the economy tanked. Your brother probably thought signing up for the Army was a way to get out of that shithole. And you ...

well, what about you? I'll be honest, I don't know much about you except your name and where you grew up."

Her body finally betrayed her; Jessica felt a tear form in the corner of her eye and start to slide down her cheek.

"Aw, look at that," Connolly said, and leaned forward, reaching for her face.

Jessica went to swat his hand away, but he was quicker. He grabbed her wrist and squeezed until she jerked and let out a small gasp of pain.

He released her and sat back in his chair, shaking his head. "You think you're the first woman that's tried to slap me?" He laughed, looking off at the two men as if to share a private joke. "Get in line."

Jessica said, "My brother did not kill himself. You killed him."

"Believe whatever you want. To be honest, I never even met your brother. I just learned tonight what happened to him, in fact. Turned out he got a taste of the product."

"That's crazy. He would never do drugs."

"Are you positive?"

She thought about Jacob's phone call, about him crying and saying he had messed up and that he was scared.

"My men are not permitted to taste the product and they are given random drug tests just to be sure they don't. After your brother's last test, he ran because he knew what we would find."

She thought about Jacob's second phone call, Jacob telling her how they were coming for him. How they were almost there, and how he was sorry and that he loved her and just wanted to hear her voice one last time.

"It didn't take long for my men to find him. They tracked him down to a motel in Arizona. He'd barricaded himself in his room. My men tried talking him out, but he knew what was going to happen once they got their hands on him, so he made it easy for himself. Put a gun in his mouth and pulled the trigger. Do you want to see the photos?"

He stared at her, waiting for a reaction, but Jessica kept her composure.

"Anyway," Connolly said, leaning forward in his seat, "that's the story of your brother's brief time of employment. But I guess it shouldn't be too surprising. He was never really employee of the month material to begin with, was he?"

Jessica couldn't contain the rage bubbling inside her any longer. She sprang up from her seat, her fingers splayed in front of her, the nails aimed at Connolly's face. She might die tonight, but she wasn't going to die without at least scarring the man, so that every time he looked in the mirror he would remember her. But she barely got out of her seat before the man behind her pushed her back down into the chair and clamped the paws of his hands on her shoulders to keep her in place.

"Really?" Connolly said, leaning back in his chair and again crossing his leg over his knee. "Is that how you want to act in the last few hours of your life?"

A chirping noise drew her attention. It was the assistant, standing off to the side. He pulled his cell phone from his pocket and turned away, placing the phone to his ear and speaking quietly.

Connolly said, "I'm still not sure how we're going to do it. We could just place a bullet in your head and bury you in the desert, but that seems boring. We could offer you the chance to kill yourself just like your brother, but I don't think you have it in you. Either way, my guys are going to have some fun with you before it's all over. I figure after the day they've had, they deserve it."

The assistant disconnected the phone and turned back around. His face appeared suddenly ashen. "Sir, we have to leave."

Connolly looked at him, annoyed. "What?"

"That was one of our contacts at the state police. He claims that there are over twenty cars headed to this location. And it's not just the police. He said there are DEA and FBI agents, too."

For the first time, Connolly looked panicked. He quickly got to his feet. "When will they be here?"

"Our contact says within a half hour, if not sooner. Sir, we have to leave *now*."

44

The road leading up to the mine was bumpy, and the Crown Vic's headlights cut the darkness in jagged swatches of light, like the ebb and flow of lines on a heart monitor. Soon the car crested the entrance to the bowl, its headlights illuminating the remains of the destroyed helicopter, then the new helicopter standing beside it. The Crown Vic made a long arc toward the entrance to the mine and the SUV and two pickups parked in front.

Two men stood off to the side, each with AR-15s slung over their shoulders. They watched the car slow and stop, and then watched the driver's door open.

"Evening, Sheriff," said one of the men. "Crazy night, ain't it?"

Nova didn't answer. He approached the men with his head tilted down so the brim of the hat obscured his face. Leonard Smith was a rotund man, so the pants and shirt were a little baggy, but he was hoping the two men wouldn't notice in the dark.

The distance between them was maybe forty yards. The men didn't speak as Nova neared them. It was only as he was twenty yards away that the man tried again.

"Sheriff?"

When Nova still didn't answer, when he didn't even lift his head up for them to see his face, the men knew something was wrong. They reached for their weapons, but the effort was in vain. Steel scraped against leather as Nova slid his sidearm from its holster and fired first at the one man, then the other man, one bullet each to the chest, never slowing his stride. The men hit the ground, still alive, and Nova stepped past them, shooting them each once more, this time in the head. He tossed the hat aside, bent and took the AR-15s from the men. He checked both loads, then strapped one of them over his shoulder, hefted the other one in both hands.

He continued up the incline into the tunnel. It was dark, with only a few lights spaced out along the walls. It curved toward the right and began to descend, and then he saw the glass door at the end.

A keypad locked the door by the handle. Leonard Smith had gladly told Nova the combination, running through the numbers at a frenzied clip as if he was relieved to get them off his chest. Nova punched the numbers as quietly as possible. A light on the keypad lit green, and a mechanical click sounded, so soft and slight it was almost like a whisper on the wind.

Nova pushed down on the handle, quietly swung the door open.

A walkway led farther into a cavern. Here the lights were bright and showed the vast production Connolly had created. A steel room with the vats and tubes of a laboratory sat in the center. Around it were several tables and chairs, computers and TVs.

Connolly and his assistant—Samuel, Leonard Smith had called him—and another man dragging Jessica were headed toward him.

For a moment nobody moved. Nobody spoke.

Then Nova raised the AR-15. "Let her go."

Connolly said, "You called the cops on me, Bartkowski?"

"It's over. You lost."

"You should know better. A true soldier never surrenders."

The group was clustered together, maybe fifty feet away. Connolly stood at the forefront, his assistant and the man holding onto Jessica behind him. No way Nova could open fire without hitting her. There was a chance, sure, but he wasn't willing to take that chance, especially with the meth lab directly behind them.

Suddenly a gun was in Connolly's hand. He yanked Jessica from the man and pointed the barrel at her head.

"Drop the weapons, Bartkowski. All of them, or I'll kill her."

Jessica didn't even struggle. She just stared back at Nova, less fear in her eyes than fury. "Don't do it."

"Shut up!" Connolly barked, pressing the barrel to her head.

The other man—not Samuel—now had a gun in his hand. He didn't raise it yet, but it was at his side, just waiting.

The lights in the ceiling of the cavern were spotlights, maybe two feet wide. There were a half dozen of them spread throughout the space.

"You kill her," Nova said, "you lose your hostage. That a wise idea?"

Connolly's gaze was steady. "I might lose my hostage, but either way she's dead."

Nova was silent for a long beat. Then he said, "Fine, you win." He held the rifle out to his side, the barrel pointed toward the ceiling. "Let her go."

"You first. Put all the weapons down."

Nova didn't move immediately. He just stared back at Jessica. He wasn't even sure what he was trying to communicate with the stare. An apology, maybe, though that might not have been it either. It didn't matter anyway. Whatever this had been, it was now over.

He looked back at Connolly. He said, "I hope you're not afraid of the dark," and opened fire at the cavern ceiling.

A lot of things happened quickly then. First one lamp went out, then a second. Shards of glass rained down everywhere. The man with the gun opened fire on Nova. Jessica, still grasped by Connolly, turned and kneed him in the groin. Connolly's grip loosened, just enough for Jessica to slip free. She started forward, toward Nova, but Connolly was turning toward her, bringing up the gun, so she bolted away in the other direction.

Nova fired at another lamp in the ceiling, then hit the ground and rolled, came back up and returned fire. One of the bullets clipped the man in the shoulder. He spun away. Beyond him, Connolly was chasing after Jessica. Samuel just stood there, weaponless, looking left and right, before taking off after his boss.

The man Nova had shot hadn't let go of his gun. As he started to raise it at Nova, Nova fired two more rounds into him.

Jessica had disappeared around the laboratory, followed by Connolly and the assistant. She cried out, and Nova heard a door slam shut. Then Connolly's voice filled the cavern.

"We're leaving now, Bartkowski. The girl's locked in the lab. You might want to get her out, or you might want to save your own ass, that's completely up to you. Because this entire place? It's rigged with C-4. We built it that way in case we ever had to destroy it fast."

As outrageous as it sounded, Nova didn't doubt the man. If Nova had constructed a multi-million dollar drug lab in the middle of nowhere, he might have done the same thing. The evidence wouldn't be completely destroyed, but it would take the authorities a very long time before they managed to retrieve anything through the rubble, and even then much of it would be compromised because of the destruction.

Connolly and Samuel were on the other side of the laboratory. Nova could see them through the glass windows. He could just as easily head back the other way, meet the two men around the other side, but he also spotted Jessica, splayed out on the floor of the lab. She was moving, slowly, sitting up and touching the side of her head, which was now fresh with blood.

"I don't have to choose," Nova said. "I can just kill you first, then save her later."

"Is that right?" Amusement in Connolly's voice. "And how are you going to get her out of the lab?"

Nova turned the corner. The first thing he saw was the table with weapons and ammunition laid out on top. Rifles, hand-guns, even a few grenades. Then he saw the door. There was a keypad by the handle, just like the keypad on the door leading into the cavern. The sheriff had only provided him with the one code, and Nova highly doubted that code opened this keypad. He tried the handle by itself, but it was locked. He punched the numbers in that had worked on the previous keypad. A red light lit up this time instead of green.

"I wouldn't punch the wrong code in more than twice," Connolly said. "Trust me, that might get … messy."

A bluff? Maybe. Right now Connolly was working for time, just enough to get himself out of the mine. He'd say or do any-thing for that to happen. But what if he was telling the truth?

Nova raised his gun at the window, but paused when he considered the chemicals inside. A stray bullet could cause tre-mendous damage. So could a ricochet. There was a reason most redneck meth labs went up in flames.

On the other side of the cavern, Nova could hear Connolly and Samuel hurry up the ramp toward the door.

He stepped around the corner, aiming at the two men.

"I wouldn't do that, Bartkowski," Connolly said, holding up the grenade in his hand. "You shoot me, I let this go, the whole thing goes up in flames. Is that what you want?"

Inside the lab, Jessica was climbing to her feet. She was hav-ing a hard time of it, keeping one hand to the side of her head to stanch the flow of blood.

Nova turned back to Connolly and Samuel, but they were

already headed up the walkway. Samuel went through the door first, and Connolly turned back, the grenade held high in his hand.

"Two minutes," Connolly said. "Enjoy them." He slipped through the door.

Nova sprinted toward the walkway. If he could get to Connolly in time, without Connolly knowing it, maybe they had a chance. Take Connolly out, even with the grenade in his hand, and at least then Connolly wouldn't have a chance to detonate the C-4 … if there even *was* C-4.

But halfway to the ramp, the door exploded. Rubble burst everywhere as the tunnel crumbled in on itself. The blast was enough to knock Nova off his feet. He hit the ground, rolled, sprang back up. Stared hard at the only exit to the cavern, as if some new door would materialize out of the debris, but the truth was clear. They were trapped.

45

Jessica had limped to the other end of the lab. She banged on the door to get Nova's attention.

"The door's locked!" she shouted through the glass.

Nova hurried over to the door. Just like the other door, a keypad secured this one.

"I don't know the code," Nova said. Then, glancing back toward the rubble: "It doesn't matter anyway."

They were quiet for a long moment. Dust fell soundlessly in the faint light.

Nova leaned his forehead against the glass, took a deep breath. "I'm sorry."

Jessica said nothing. She kept her hand against the side of her head, but the blood kept coming.

Suddenly her eyes lit up. "There's another way."

"What?"

"Out of the mine." Excitement in her voice. "There's another way out of the mine!"

"How?"

"First, can you get me out of here?"

Nova looked around. From the rubble of the explosion he retrieved the largest rock he could handle. He crossed to one of the wide windows on the side of the lab, one where there didn't appear to be much equipment, and lifted the rock above his head.

The glass didn't shatter like he had hoped it would, but it did crack. The rock bounced off and hit the ground.

Nova picked it back up and threw it again. Still no shatter, but the pane of glass spiderwebbed even more.

The third time was the charm.

Pieces of glass fell everywhere. Nova used the barrel of the AR-15 to dislodge any loose shards sticking up out of the frame, then tossed the rifle aside. Jessica hobbled up and held out her arms. Nova reached over the broken window and picked her up and out of the lab.

"We don't have much time," he said. "Connolly's going to blow this place."

She was already limping toward the back of the cavern. "I did research on this mine, remember? They actually built two entrances."

The concrete floor fell away as the pipes continued to snake into the darkness. Nova pulled the flashlight from his belt. He turned it on, handed it to Jessica.

"Hold this," he said, and picked her up.

They continued forward as quickly as they could, Nova carrying Jessica as she shined the flashlight ahead of them. The pipes went deeper and deeper into the mine. Fortunately there was enough room for Nova and Jessica to squeeze through. Then the tunnel turned left and they began to ascend.

Nova pushed himself as hard as he could.

They went around a curve and suddenly Jessica's flashlight showed them only darkness. The pipes just stopped. But no, that wasn't right—something was sealing the exit. The pipes disappeared through what appeared to be a solid wall.

Nova set Jessica down.

When she spoke, her voice was soft and full of defeat. "Now what?"

He took the flashlight from her and approached the wall. It was painted black. He tapped his fist against it and heard the hollow echo of wood.

"It's plywood," he said. "Judging by the sound, it's one or two inches thick."

"Can you break it down?"

Nova stepped back, handing Jessica the flashlight. "Move away and cover your ears."

"What are you going to do?"

Nova unslung the other AR-15 from around his shoulder and aimed it at the door. "The only thing I can do right now."

"How much more time do you think we have?"

Nova didn't get a chance to answer. At that moment the ground began to shake. It was a slight tremor at first, like a minor earthquake, and then the world exploded farther down the tunnel.

Time was up.

46

Connolly led them out of the tunnel, both he and Samuel running, the grenade behind them having just exploded.

It was a stupid, rash decision on Connolly's part, but so what? He knew he was only human, was as fallible as anybody else, and he was *pissed*. Everything—his entire empire—had crumbled away in the matter of only hours. And it was all because of that son of a bitch Bartkowski.

Connolly wasn't surprised to see the two men dead outside the mine entrance, but he was surprised to see Leonard Smith's Crown Vic. He wondered briefly what had become of his uncle. Then he shook it off. On a sinking ship, it was every man for himself.

They headed for the helicopter.

"Where's the pilot?" Connolly asked.

Samuel hesitated. "You said you wanted as many men as possible searching the desert."

Connolly gritted his teeth but said nothing, keeping his focus on the approaching chopper.

Samuel asked, "Should we contact the rest of the men?"

Connolly didn't even pause to consider the question. "No, keep them out there. The more scattered they are, the more of a headache it will be for the police."

Samuel said nothing to this, but Connolly could tell the man didn't approve.

Connolly stopped and grabbed a fistful of the man's shirt. "Do you have a problem?"

Samuel stared right back at him, his face impassive. "No."

"No what?"

"No, sir."

Connolly didn't move for several seconds, his gaze heavy on Samuel's, until the man blinked and looked away. Good. Dominance was established once again. As it should be.

He let go of Samuel's shirt and continued on toward the helicopter.

Samuel stood still for a moment, then hurried to keep pace beside him. "There's a good chance they won't find out about you right away. We should be able to leave the country before that happens."

They stepped through the shadows of the helicopter's frozen rotor blades.

Connolly nodded as he opened the door. "We'll make the call once we're in the air. But I want to make one stop before we leave the country completely."

Connolly stepped up into the helicopter, slammed the door shut. Samuel hustled to the other side. Connolly already had his earphones on, was checking the gauges, flipping switches. The engine kicked on and the rotor blades began to make their rotation, slow at first but picking up speed.

Connolly pointed at the phone in Samuel's hand. "Type in the number."

Samuel didn't need to be told what number that was. There was only one number that Connolly could possibly mean under the circumstances. The C-4 throughout the mine was already primed and ready to go. Had been since the lab was first established five years ago. Only one number would detonate it, a number only Connolly and Samuel knew.

Samuel dialed the number.

As soon as the rotors were going fast enough, Connolly pulled back on the stick. The helicopter began to rise into the air. They crested the bowl and then kept going higher. Connolly wanted to make sure they were far enough away from the blast zone. He also wanted to get a good view of the explosion. Not that they would see much in the dark, but the fact Barkowski was inside made it a nice consolation.

Samuel had inputted the number and was now waiting for the order to press SEND.

"Do it," Connolly said.

Samuel pressed his thumb to the green button. For a moment nothing happened, and then the side of the bowl began to shake and ripple and fall in on itself. Pieces of rubble exploded out of the mine entrance and rained down on the parked vehicles. A cloud of dirt and dust rose up into the air.

Connolly waited for another moment—memorizing the destruction, savoring it—before adjusting the stick and pointing them west.

47

The AR-15's magazine contained thirty .223 Remington caliber rounds. Nova emptied the entire magazine in a matter of seconds, starting at the center of the board before spraying the top and bottom and sides. Then he threw the rifle aside, sprinted at the wall, and threw all his weight into the barrier.

He broke through.

Jessica hurriedly limped after him just as the tunnel began to collapse. Nova grabbed her and pulled her away. They were outside now, on the side of a hill. Nova slipped and fell and rolled several yards down the incline before managing to stop himself.

"Are you all right?" Jessica shouted.

He picked himself up, dusted off his hands, and looked at how much farther it was to level ground. Nodding, he said, "We need keep going."

Jessica limped up next to him. Nova went to pick her up again, but she shook her head and told him no, she didn't want to be carried anymore.

Nova squinted at the gash on the side of her head. "Is that still bleeding?"

She touched the wound gingerly, her fingers coming away covered in fresh blood.

Nova unbuttoned the sheriff's shirt and slipped it off his shoulders. He wrapped it around her head and used the sleeves to tie it tight. It wasn't perfect but it did the trick.

"Now what?" Jessica asked.

"Now we head back to the entrance. Hopefully the sheriff's car wasn't destroyed in the blast."

"Why?"

"I have the sheriff locked in the trunk."

They started around the hill toward the entrance to the bowl. Because of Jessica's leg and her insistence to walk on her own, it took them a while but that was okay. Right now nobody was chasing them. Connolly's men were still over in Kadrey searching the desert. Maybe they had heard the explosion, but Nova doubted it. He also doubted any of the men would contact Connolly. After all, it wasn't like they would have news that they had found Nova. None of the men would want to admit they hadn't been successful yet. The only communication would come from Connolly himself, and Nova doubted Connolly had warned his men about the approaching authorities.

Fifteen minutes later they crested the top of the ridge and started down into the bowl. Even in the faint moonlight they could see the entrance to the mine had been destroyed.

The helicopter was gone.

The vehicles—or what was left of the vehicles—were all covered in a layer of dust and rubble. The Crown Vic hadn't been completely destroyed in the blast. The windshield had been shattered, but that appeared to be the worst of the damage.

Nova still had the key in his pocket. He slipped it out as they approached the trunk.

Jessica stopped him, placing a hand on his arm. "Thank you," she said.

"For what?"

"You didn't have to do this for me."

"Who says I did it for you?"

She smiled. "That's right. You're in love with that coworker of yours."

Nova decided to ignore that. "What about you? Did you find what you were looking for?"

She was quiet for a moment, her gaze focused at something distant over his shoulder. "Not really. It turns out my brother wasn't really who I thought he was."

"What do you mean?"

"Connolly told me he became addicted. That's why he got in trouble. He wasn't trying to bring these people to justice. He just got hooked on meth. He ran, and Connolly's men chased him. My brother …" She shook her head, her voice cracking. "Connolly's men didn't kill Jacob. Jacob killed himself."

Nova used his finger to tilt her face toward him. She didn't want to at first, keeping her gaze glued on that distant spot over his shoulder.

"Hey," he said.

She looked at him.

"Fuck Connolly. The guy's a prick. Are you really going to believe anything he told you?"

Jessica didn't answer.

"You know your brother cared about you a lot, don't you?"

A slight nod.

"He blew off a hot date and drove three hours to visit you at camp, didn't he?"

Another slight nod.

"That happened. Connolly can't take that away from you. Nobody can take that away from you. Your brother loved you more than anything. That's all that matters."

Up over the top of the bowl came the crunch of gravel and engines. Flashing red and blue lights winked off in the distance.

Nova inserted the key, popped the trunk. Sheriff Leonard

Smith lay inside, his wrists handcuffed behind his back, a gag in his mouth. He wore only his underwear and undershirt and socks.

Smith stared up at them, grunted something indistinguishable.

"What's that?" Nova said. "You want me to keep you locked in there?"

Smith grunted even more loudly, his eyes wide in protest.

"Don't worry. I'm not locking you up anymore. These guys, on the other hand …"

He stepped back as the first car crested the ridge. Even in the dark Nova could see the state trooper logo on the side of the vehicle.

Nova pulled the only weapons he had left on his person—a handgun and knife—and tossed them on the ground.

"We should probably make it easy on them," he said.

"What do you mean?"

Nova showed her. He lowered himself to his knees, threaded his fingers and placed his hands on the back of his head.

Jessica lowered herself to her knees and did the same.

Neither of them spoke then, both waiting, and watched three more police cars follow the first one down into the bowl, their rooftop reds and blues lighting up the night like a disco.

48

All three of them—Sheriff Leonard Smith included—were searched and handcuffed. The troopers didn't say much other than to ask if they were hurt. Smith started in about how he was the sheriff and how he shouldn't be the one in cuffs, but the troopers ignored him and placed him in the back of one of the cars. Another trooper checked Jessica's ankle, then the gash on the side of her head. He wrapped her head in gauze before putting her in the back of another car and driving her away.

Nova asked, "Where are they taking her?"

"There's an ambulance right now in Kadrey," one of the troopers said. "Now, what's your name?"

Nova said nothing.

The trooper didn't look happy about it, but he also didn't look surprised. He led Nova to the third car and put him in the backseat.

Nova watched the men search the other vehicles, inspect the dead bodies, and climb up over the rubble where the mine entrance used to be. After a while the troopers converged and spoke. A few glanced at Nova and Smith in their separate cars, but none of the troopers approached either car.

It was about twenty minutes before the helicopter arrived. Unlike Connolly's private helicopters, this one was a UH-72 Lakota, primarily used by the U.S. Army. It flew over the top of the bowl and circled, its turboshaft engines and rotors thrumming the air while its lights searched the ground for a safe place to land.

The troopers shifted away, shielding their eyes with their hands, as the helicopter set down near the wreckage of the other chopper.

Soon the Lakota was powering down and an old man with glasses and white hair exited. He approached the troopers as the troopers approached him. Hands were shook, words were spoken, heads tilted either up and down or back and forth. Finally one of the troopers turned and pointed at Leonard Smith, then at Nova. The old man peered at Nova for a long moment before saying a few more words to the men. One of the troopers placed something in the man's hand. The man nodded his thanks and then started in Nova's direction.

He walked around to the other side of the car and opened the door.

"Casanova Bartkowski?"

"My friends call me Nova."

"We need to talk."

The man slid into the back and shut the door.

"Here," the man said, holding up a key, "let me undo those cuffs for you."

Nova shifted in the seat so his bound wrists were aimed toward the man. The man inserted the key and unlocked the cuffs.

"Thanks," Nova said. "So who are you?"

"My name's Winters. I believe you and I share a mutual friend."

"Atticus."

"That's right. I don't hear from him much anymore, so when I do hear from him, I know it's important. And he calls me tonight about a problem out in Nevada. Says someone he knows is in trouble."

"They were cooking meth inside the mine."

"Who was?"

"Everyone in town, from what I understand. The sheriff over there will give you the whole story. At least he sang like a bird for me. Mostly everyone in town is military, working as either security or transportation. Besides them there are a few chemists. They all worked in shifts, ten hours a day, seven days a week."

"Jesus," Winters said quietly. Then, staring out his window at the rubble: "What happened to the mine?"

"The guy in charge had it rigged with C-4. Blew it up when he got out of here."

"Do you know his name?"

"All I ever heard him called was Connolly. You'll be able to get more out of the sheriff. Connolly's actually his nephew."

"How long ago did he leave?"

"Maybe an hour ago. There was another helicopter here. They must have left in it."

"Any idea where he was headed?"

Nova didn't answer.

Winters said, "Mr. Bartkowski, you are not currently under trial. Atticus vouches for you, so as far as I'm concerned you get a free pass."

"The girl, too."

"What's that?"

"The girl should get a free pass, too. She has nothing to do with any of this. Just in the wrong place at the wrong time."

"I understand. But keep in mind what happens to her is out of my hands."

"Do you want to catch Connolly?"

"We'll catch him."

"You might not. He could be on a plane out of the country as we speak."

"We're monitoring all the airports on the west coast, both major and minor. No wheels go up without our say so. What exactly happened here?"

"Do you want to catch Connolly?"

"We'll catch him."

"First, nothing happens to the girl. I don't want her name involved. She gets fixed up at the hospital and goes home without even a lecture."

Winters was quiet for a moment, thinking something over. "Fine, nothing happens to the girl. Now what about Connolly?"

"Before he tries to leave the country, I think he's going to make one stop."

"What makes you say that?"

"I've known men like him, and they're all the same—prideful but also spiteful."

"How would I go about finding this man?"

"The deal is I would find him for you."

Winters was quiet for another several long seconds. Finally he asked, "How?"

"That depends," Nova said. He nodded at the Lakota. "How fast can that thing fly?"

49

This section of the Pacific Coast Highway wasn't busy at this time of the morning. As they sped south with the ocean on their right, the sun was just beginning to peek up over the horizon. The traffic was sparse, a few cars and tractor-trailers here and there, but that was it.

They drove in silence. Not that it was unusual for them to be together in silence. Samuel wasn't a friend, and Connolly had never pretended he was. Samuel was his employee, plain and simple. The man was expendable. Once this was over, Connolly would see to it that he was eliminated. Connolly might even do it himself. Obviously he had become too lax in his current position. This never would have happened years ago when he first started building his empire.

His empire. Shit. How long it took to build and how quickly it fell, all because of one asshole.

But that was okay. They were going to take care of that right now. Not that it mattered much in the larger scheme of things—the asshole was dead, buried under a ton of rubble—but at least it would make Connolly feel better, and after everything that had happened, he wanted to feel good about something.

Samuel had made the appropriate calls in the helicopter. First about a private jet to take them out of the country, then about making a visit to the garage or warehouse or wherever the fuck they kept the cars. Samuel got confirmation on both. In fact, the jet they needed was just past the place in which they would find Casanova Bartkowski's Mustang. So they landed at one airport, secured a car, and had been driving now for two hours. In another hour they would be in the air, headed toward Asia.

But first the Mustang.

At some point Samuel turned off the highway. The road was worn and ragged, dirt filling the cracks and sending up a cloud of dust in their wake.

After several miles of open fields they came to an abandoned warehouse. It was the only structure for at least a mile. A chain-link fence ran the perimeter, razor wire curving on top. A large weathered sign near the gate said PRIVATE PROPERTY KEEP OUT.

Samuel slowed the sedan in front of the gate. He put the car in park and kept the engine idling.

Connolly said, "Now what?"

Samuel hit the horn.

A man stepped out of the warehouse. He squinted at them for a long moment, then hurried over. He inserted a key into the padlock on the gate, and pushed the gate open.

The man chased after them as Samuel drove toward the building. He parked the sedan in front. Connolly and Samuel got out of the car just as the man caught up with them.

"Where is it?" Connolly said.

The man motioned them inside.

Connolly pulled a gun from his pocket. "No fucking around, right?"

The man's eyes grew wide at the sight of the gun. "What?

No way, man. You want me to show you the car, I'll show you the car."

Connolly followed the man inside the warehouse. It smelled like a warehouse should. Dust and oil and gasoline. Cars were everywhere. Many of them were already being taken apart. Others would be sent overseas and sold to the highest bidder.

"Where is everyone?" Connolly asked as the man led them deeper into the warehouse.

"It's six o'clock in the morning," the man said. "People are in bed. The only reason I'm here is because I got a call an hour ago telling me to meet you here."

The man took them toward the rear corner of the warehouse where the Mustang was parked. Its tires, which had been shot and shredded, had since been replaced.

The man cleared his throat. "I'm supposed to remind you just how much this car costs."

Connolly said, "Is that right? Then maybe I should remind you the operation that brought this car here was done without my permission. One would think to know better than to do things without my permission."

He said it to the man but knew his words hit Samuel the hardest.

Without another word Connolly approached the Mustang and raised the gun at the windshield.

Behind him, a voice said, "Don't."

At first Connolly thought it was the man. The voice certainly didn't sound like Samuel's. But then the voice spoke again—"Put it down, asshole"—and Connolly's blood went cold.

He turned, slowly, looking first at Samuel, then at the man, then at Casanova Bartkowski standing only a few yards away. Bartkowski had a gun in his own hand. He wasn't aiming it at Connolly, but Connolly knew that didn't matter. He knew that if Bartkowski wanted to, he could place a bullet between Connolly's eyes in less than a second.

"You're supposed to be dead."

Bartkowski shrugged. "Sorry to disappoint."

As if on cue, a dozen more men appeared around the warehouse. They all wore black tactical gear, much like the kind Connolly's men had worn last night, and each had assault rifles aimed at Connolly.

"I know what you're thinking," Bartkowski said. "You're thinking if you raise that gun of yours, these men will take you down. You'll go out in a blaze of glory and won't have to spend the rest of your life in prison."

"What makes you think I'll go to prison?"

"Your uncle spilled his guts to me in five minutes. Told me the whole operation, front to back. Just imagine what he'll tell the authorities."

"It's his word against mine."

"And your men?"

"What men?"

"The truth is," Bartkowski said, "I don't see you going to prison. I don't even see you going to trial. The people above you—your investors—will never take the chance you'll turn on them."

Connolly said nothing.

"They got people everywhere. It doesn't matter where you go, they'll find you. You could promise to flip right now and want to enter WITSEC, but they would still find you. I wouldn't be surprised after the shit that just went down in Parrot Spur, they're not looking for you already. They already know you're planning to leave the country. The authorities already have every airport in California on high alert. It didn't take long at all to find the private jet you were planning to use. Even if you had bypassed this place completely, you never would have gotten off the ground. But a hunch told me you would stop here first. And look what happened—you now have a dozen men aiming weapons at you. So drop the gun, get down on your knees, and put your hands on your head."

Connolly stood motionless. His fingers tightened around the rubber pistol grip. His gaze swept the warehouse, from Bartkowski to the men surrounding them and then back to Bartkowski. Samuel and the man who had led them in here had seemingly disappeared. They were not important. What was important now was Bartkowski and those men in tactical gear. And the gun in Connolly's hand.

"Don't," Bartkowski said. "I can see it in your eyes what you're thinking. And trust me, nothing would please me more than to place a bullet in your head. Now drop the gun and get down on your knees."

Connolly's grip on the gun tightened even more. His gaze swept the warehouse again. This time Samuel and the man who had led them in here reappeared. He saw Samuel watching him. Waiting to see what Connolly would do. Connolly wouldn't be in this position if it wasn't for Samuel. If anything, *Samuel* was the one who had brought everything to this point. *Samuel* was the one who needed to die.

"Do you want me to count to ten?" Bartkowski said.

"Don't bother."

The gun slipped through Connolly's fingers, fell to the concrete floor. His glare burning into Barkowski, he lowered himself to his knees and placed his hands on the back of his head.

The men in tactical gear advanced. Connolly was thrown to the ground, quickly searched, and secured with zip-ties. They pulled him to his feet and pushed him toward the front of the warehouse.

As he passed Bartkowski, Connolly said, "This isn't over yet."

Bartkowski didn't even blink. "Yes it is."

50

It felt weird being back behind the wheel. It hadn't even been two days and already the Mustang felt like it belonged to someone else. But it drove just fine, even with the four new tires, and Nova followed the PCH for a half hour before he realized just how hungry he was. He hadn't eaten anything in nearly twenty-four hours. It hadn't been a problem before because his body had been on full alert, but now his stomach was beginning to growl.

A gas station was coming up on the right. He flicked on his turn signal and eased his way into the parking lot.

His goal had been to drive across the country, and now here he was in California, the smell of the Pacific Ocean thick in the air. Despite this, he felt no satisfaction.

He stepped through the door into the air conditioning, a bell jangling above his head.

The kid behind the counter looked up from his magazine, paused at the sight of Nova's face and clothes, and then slowly nodded hello.

"Bathroom?" Nova asked.

The kid jerked a thumb toward the rear of the store.

Nova headed down the aisles, thinking he might get some candy bars and a soda. Junk food, sure, but it would be something to hold him over until he got wherever he was going. He would need to stop someplace for clothes first. His clothes were filthy. Blood spotted his jeans. He was pretty sure most of the blood didn't belong to him.

In the bathroom he stared at himself in the mirror. No wonder the kid had looked scared. Nova was a mess. He felt like it, too, but that was nothing new. Or was it?

Shaking his head, he turned on the faucet and pressed the button for soap. The odor hit him at once, just as the orange dollop touched his palm. Dial soap.

Nova didn't move for several long seconds, the water from the spout running. Finally he blinked and washed his hands. He grabbed a paper towel, dried his hands, turned off the water, and headed back into the store.

The kid was still behind the counter, watching him. Nova didn't slow in any of the aisles. He didn't pluck any candy bars from the wire racks. He went straight for the door. The bell jangled again above his head as he stepped outside.

He used his key to pop the trunk. A crowbar lay inside. He pulled it out, held it in his hand for a moment, then swung it back over his head.

The rear windshield spiderwebbed on the first hit. On the second the glass broke and rained inside. Nova went to the rear side window next, then the front side window. Swinging the crowbar again and again. Glass popping and shattering. Metal crunching and tearing. Nova didn't stop. His breathing was calm. His pulse had slowed. He was in a zone, thinking about nothing else except Dial soap washing young hands after having washed and fed and helped a dying woman to the bathroom. And this car—this Mustang that he had always cherished, had always coveted, had always known that one day would be his despite his old man telling him it would never happen—needed to be destroyed. It needed to be taken apart, piece by piece, though Nova didn't have the patience for that. And so he swung the crowbar, again and again, circling the car a second time, the crowbar held high over his head for yet another crushing blow when the kid shouted at him.

"The hell are you doing?"

Nova paused, the crowbar tight in his hand, and tilted his face toward the kid.

The kid took a slow, hesitant step back.

"It's okay," Nova said. "It's my car."

"What?"

"The car. I own it. I can do whatever the fuck I want with it."

"But … you're making a mess."

Nova dropped his shoulders, let the crowbar clatter to the ground. He reached into his pocket and pulled out several fifty-dollar bills. Winters had given them to him before they parted ways. For gas, Winters had said. Nova started to approach the kid, but the kid started to back away again.

"I'm not going to hurt you," Nova said.

"Yeah, sure. Is that what you told your car?"

Nova counted out ten of the fifties and extended them to the kid. "Call a tow truck. Have them take the car wherever they want. Smash it up, fix it up, I don't care. I don't want it anymore."

The kid still looked hesitant, but he took the proffered fifties. "What about my parking lot?"

Nova glanced again at what was left of the Mustang. Bent and broken metal and shards of glass glinting in the morning sunlight. He counted out two more fifties and handed them to the kid.

The kid took the bills but said nothing.

"Where's the closest Walmart?"

The kid pointed down the highway.

"Thanks," Nova said.

He started walking.

CODA

He walked several miles before he reached the Walmart. Inside he purchased some clothes and a charger for his iPhone as well as a knapsack. He continued down the highway another several miles before he came to a motel. The clerk inside told him they had one vacancy, a room that overlooked the ocean. Nova said he'd take it.

The room was nothing special. He dumped the contents of the knapsack out on the bed. He plugged the charger into his phone and waited for it to power up. The Apple logo appeared, and then a minute later the phone was up and running with a full signal. Nova waited for notifications, but none popped up. No voicemails. No text messages. No emails. Nothing.

He stripped out of his clothes and stepped into the shower. He stood under the water for a long time, his eyes closed. His muscles were sore and tender from the past twenty-four hours. Dirt had embedded itself in his skin, and he had to scrub harder than usual to rid himself of the filth.

Out of the shower then, he dried off and wrapped the towel

around his waist. He thought about dressing, but his eyelids were growing heavy.

He didn't bother pulling up the comforter. He lay on top and folded his hands over his chest and closed his eyes. Outside he could hear the soft shushing of waves hitting the beach. The distant cries of seagulls. The faint and frenzied laughter of children as they raced across the sand.

On the bedside table, his cell phone vibrated.

Nova opened his eyes.

The cell phone vibrated again.

Nova sat up and threw his feet off the bed and onto the floor. He stared down at the cell phone as it continued to vibrate with an incoming call.

Nobody had this number. He had changed phones once he left D.C. Wanted to cut ties completely. The only one who might call him was the phone company, but he doubted they were conducting a follow-up to see whether or not he was satisfied with his service.

The phone kept vibrating.

On the screen it said BLOCKED.

Nova picked up the phone.

"Hello?"

"How are you feeling?"

The voice didn't sound familiar at first. Then, frowning, Nova said, "Atticus?"

"Winters was impressed with your work. I told him I wasn't surprised."

"I hope he kept up his end of the bargain."

"The girl? Yes, she'll be taken care of. How's your vacation treating you?"

"Why are you calling?"

Atticus hesitated. "It's Holly."

"What's wrong? Is she okay?"

"She's fine. Well, as fine as one can be under the circumstances."

The last time Nova saw Holly Lin she was standing over three dead bodies in an elevator. One of those bodies belonged to Javier Diaz. It was because of Javier Diaz that Holly had gone to Mexico. A threat had been placed against her family, and the only way to ensure her family's safety was to kill Javier's father and everyone else in the family.

"Is she hurt?" Nova asked.

"I said she's fine, Nova, and I mean it."

"Is this about Diaz?"

"No. This is another matter. Something ... more complex."

"Meaning?"

Another hesitation on Atticus's end. Nova didn't know the man very well, but this seemed out of character.

Finally Atticus said, "Meaning she needs your help."

"She's still in Mexico?"

"Yes."

"Where?"

"Culiacán."

Nova rose from the bed and crossed the room to the window overlooking the beach. He watched the people down there, the families and children and couples, and wondered what it was like to enjoy a nice sunny day at the beach. It was because of people like Nova—and Holly Lin—that those families and children and couples were able to take time out of their hectic lives to enjoy themselves on the sand. And Nova, for some reason he still wasn't sure why, had walked away from it all.

"What does she need my help with?"

This time Atticus spoke with no hesitation.

"To stop a serial killer."

ABOUT THE AUTHOR

Robert Swartwood is the *USA Today* bestselling author of *The Serial Killer's Wife*, *The Calling*, *Man of Wax*, and several other novels. He created the term "hint fiction" and is the editor of *Hint Fiction: An Anthology of Stories in 25 Words or Fewer*. He lives with his wife in Pennsylvania.

Printed in Great Britain
by Amazon